Room for Dreams

Annika Stone

Room for Dreams

Chapter One

The welding torch hissed to life at 5:47 AM, its blue-white flame casting dancing shadows across the walls of Katie Carter's workshop-slash-garage. Sparks cascaded like falling stars, each one a tiny rebellion against the pre-dawn darkness pressing against the windows. The air tasted of hot metal and hope, though lately, Katie had been choking on the latter.

She adjusted her helmet and leaned into the work, guiding molten metal along the seam of what would—eventually, hopefully, maybe—become her breakthrough piece. The one that would finally make some gallery director see past "technically proficient" to "visionary." The one that would prove she was more than just Liam Carter's little sister who made nice garden sculptures for tourists.

The metal sang under her torch, different notes for different moods. This morning it hummed low and uncertain, matching the restless energy that had driven her from bed at four in the morning. Again. She'd given up counting the nights when sleep felt less important than the desperate need to create something that mattered.

Through the open garage door, a cool breeze from across the lake and over the pine trees swept across her sweat-dampened neck. April in Northern Michigan meant unpredictable weather, the promise of spring wrestling with winter's reluctance to leave. Soon the roads would begin to fill with the early waves of down-state visitors seeking their slice of "authentic" Up North charm. They'd buy her wind chimes and garden stakes, tell her how "talented" she was, take selfies with her larger pieces.

None of them would know she'd been rejected by fourteen galleries in two years.

Minutes later, hours maybe, Katie pulled back from the sculpture. She flipped up her helmet to study the form emerging from raw metal. It was supposed to be abstract—a meditation on isolation and connection, according to her artist's statement for this series. But even she could see it was becoming another lighthouse.

She always ended up making lighthouses when her mind wandered.

"Dammit." She killed the torch and yanked off her gloves, throwing them onto the workbench cluttered with sketches, welding rods and wire, and the cold coffee she'd forgotten about an hour ago. The mug—chipped, its "Welcome to Chi-Town" lettering fading—had been given to her back when everything seemed possible. Before Mom's cancer took over their lives. Graham had given her a matching set the week before she left for art school. "One to take, one to come home to," he'd said, his careful expression barely masking something deeper. She'd left the second mug untouched in its box all these years.

Five years. Had it really been five years since she'd come home from Chicago? Just for a few months, she'd said. Just until Mom was better.

The workshop—actually her brother Liam's garage—held the evidence of those five years like a museum of almosts. Photographs from her Interlochen days, when she'd been the golden girl headed for greatness. Her acceptance letter to the Art Institute, now yellowed and pinned between a purchase order for steel and a past-due notice from the welding supply company. The first-edition book on metalwork techniques Graham had somehow found for her twenty-fifth birthday, when she'd mentioned missing the Art Institute's library.

Sketches for pieces that would revolutionize modern metal sculpture—if she could just get someone to look past her zip code.

The metal lighthouse mocked her from the workbench, its form too perfect, too safe. Too much like something Liam's little sister would make.

The crunch of tires on gravel broke through her spiral of self-pity. Chuck's mail truck, earlier than usual. Katie's stomach clenched even before she saw the thin envelope in his hand as he climbed out.

"Morning, Katie!" Chuck had been delivering mail in Green Arbor for thirty years and had never met an emotional boundary he couldn't cheerfully cross. "Envelope from the city. Thought you'd want it right away."

The return address—Minneapolis Arts Collective—made her hands shake as she took it. This was the one. The gallery that understood contemporary vision. The curator who'd seemed genuinely excited by her portfolio.

"Thanks, Chuck." Her voice sounded normal. That was good.

He lingered, clearly hoping for news to spread at Maisie's diner later. But something in her face must have warned him off because he retreated to his truck with only a sympathetic, "Maybe I should've waited."

Katie stood in her driveway, still in her welding

leathers despite the morning chill, and opened her fifteenth rejection.

Dear Ms. Carter,

Thank you for submitting your portfolio to the Minneapolis Arts Collective. While your work demonstrates technical proficiency and admirable craftsmanship, we feel it lacks the unique artistic vision we seek for our contemporary exhibitions...

The words blurred. Same phrases, different letterhead. Technically proficient. Admirable craftsmanship. Lacks vision.

Behind her, still cooling on the workbench, the metal lighthouse began to warp. The careful seams she'd just welded split with a sound like ice cracking. The abstract base—her meditation on isolation—melted into something else entirely. By the time Katie turned around, her morning's work had transformed into a slag that looked like a ragged upraised fist. With one finger up.

"What the hell?" She stared at the impossible sculpture. Metal didn't do that. Metal followed rules, responded to heat and pressure in predictable ways. It didn't reshape itself based on the artist's emotional state.

Graham would probably say something philosophical about art becoming what it was meant to be, not what the artist intended. He'd look at her with those steady eyes, head tilted just slightly, the way he did when considering a rare book. Like he was seeing something worth his full attention.

Except, sometimes, here in Green Arbor, impossible things happened. Most of the really crazy stuff happened up at the Starlight Arbor Inn. Doors locking themselves, old music playing, lost rings found years later sitting on a tabletop, that sort of thing. But whatever powered up the crazy at the Inn must travel underground. Katie had seen plenty weird in town, and sometimes out here, too.

But it never seemed to help her.

She slumped onto her work stool, rejection letter crumpling in her fist. The workshop suddenly felt too small, too full of failed dreams and statements of artistic inadequacy. She needed air. She needed coffee that wasn't cold. She needed to stop making lighthouses when she was supposed to be revolutionizing contemporary metal sculpture.

"You're up early. Again."

Katie didn't jump anymore when Ella appeared. Her sister-in-law, on feet soft as a lynx's, had developed an uncanny ability to materialize exactly when needed, usually carrying food. This morning was no exception. Ella stood in the workshop doorway with a wicker basket that smelled like Beatrice's legendary blueberry muffins.

Katie looked at her watch. "It's seven," she said. "That's not early."

"It is when you've probably been working since four." Ella stepped carefully around welding equipment and rejected dreams, setting the basket on the only clear surface. Five months of marriage to Liam had given her the comfortable glow of a woman who'd found her home, and nearly a year of running the Starlight Arbor Inn had given her the confidence of someone who'd made peace with everyday magic. "I saw your lights from the inn."

"Checking up on me?"

"The inn suggested I bring breakfast." Ella unpacked muffins, a thermos of actual hot coffee, and what looked suspiciously like Agnes's secret-recipe jam. "I'm just the delivery service."

Katie wanted to maintain her armor of sarcasm, but the coffee smelled too good and Ella's concern was too genuine. "Minneapolis said no."

"Oh, honey." Ella's hand covered hers, warm and steady. "I'm sorry."

"Fifteen galleries, Ella. Fifteen. You know what they all say? 'Technically proficient but lacks vision.' Like I'm some kind of really talented hobbyist." Katie gestured at the warped lighthouse. "And now my metal's having opinions about my life choices."

Ella studied the sculpture. "It makes quite the statement."

"It's supposed to be abstract."

"Maybe it is. Maybe it's abstractly telling you something." Ella poured coffee, added the obscene amount of sugar Katie preferred, and handed over the Starlight blue-and-white mug like a peace offering. "Speaking of lighthouses..."

"No."

"You don't even know what I was going to say."

"Yes, I do. Graham mentioned it at the last town meeting. The lighthouse keeper position. Tour guide meets groundskeeper meets historical interpreter. I'm an artist, Ella, not a—"

"Not a what? Not someone who deserves steady income and health insurance and an actual art studio?" Ella's voice stayed gentle, but her words hit their marks. "The position includes the keeper's cottage. The basement has been converted to an artist's workspace. Lake views, more square footage than this garage, and no neighbors to complain about the noise."

Katie's automatic rejection stalled in her throat. A real studio. Steady income. Space to work without wondering if she could afford next month's propane delivery.

"I'd have to give tours," she said weakly.

"Three days a week during summer. Weekends only in winter. The rest of the time would be yours." Ella pulled a folded paper from the basket—of course she'd brought the job posting. "The application deadline is end of April. That's less than two weeks. The selection committee wants someone who understands Green Arbor's history and values. Someone who sees the lighthouse as more than just a tourist attraction."

"Someone local, you mean."

"Someone who belongs here."

The words shouldn't have stung, but they did. Katie had spent five years trying to prove she belonged somewhere else—Chicago, New York, anywhere but the small Michigan town where she'd always be Liam's little sister. But here was Ella, glowing with the contentment of choosing to stay, suggesting that belonging somewhere wasn't the same as being trapped there.

"I'll think about it," Katie heard herself say.

Ella's smile was carefully neutral, but Katie caught the gleam of satisfaction in her eyes.

"Graham's on the selection committee," Ella added casually, repacking the basket. "Historical Society representative."

Katie snorted, ignoring the odd flutter in her chest. "Of course he is. Captain Careful probably has a whole binder of lighthouse regulations. Color-coded." The words came out sharper than intended, like she was trying to convince herself of something.

"He did seem very... thorough at the last meeting." Ella's tone was too innocent. "Made sure they ordered all the right research materials for candidates. Even found some rare book about lighthouse construction techniques. Special ordered it from downstate."

"Thrilling." The word tasted bitter. But something nagged at Katie's memory. Graham's eyes had lit up when she'd mentioned that manual at the bookstore last month, the way they did when he talked about first editions or community history. Like he saw magic in things other people overlooked. And he hadn't told her he'd ordered it.

"Well, I should get back." Ella paused at the open garage door. "Inn's fully booked starting Friday. Early birds this year. Summer season officially kicks off."

"Let me guess. Time for my annual parade of vacation flings?" Katie managed a grin, but it felt hollow. It was easier to joke about her tendency to have brief, passionate affairs with summer people than to examine why she only chose men who'd be gone by Labor Day. Men who didn't know about all her rejections, all her failures. Men who couldn't compare her to the golden girl she'd once been, the way certain bookstore owners with perfect memories could.

"Investment banker from Chicago, actually. Checked in last night. Very handsome. Very divorced." Ella's eyes danced. "Want me to arrange an accidental meeting?"

"Maybe." It had been... what, eight months since her last fling? Too long. Too much time focused on metal and rejection letters. Maybe what she needed was someone to remind her she was a woman, not just a failing artist. Someone who'd leave before things got complicated. Before she had to be seen as more than Katie-who-welds-and-looks-good-in-cutoffs.

After Ella left, Katie sat in her workshop staring at the former-lighthouse sculpture. Her phone buzzed. Chicago area code.

Heard about Minneapolis. Ridiculous. Your work is fire 🔥

Tony, from her Art Institute days. Still fighting the good fight in the city, still sending her gallery leads that never panned out. Another text followed immediately.

BTW, friend's gallery in NYC looking for emerging artists. Want intro?

Katie stared at the messages. Same promises, different city. How many introductions had led nowhere? How many "emerging artist" opportunities had emerged into nothing but more rejection letters to turn face-down?

She didn't respond. Instead, she found herself outside, hiking up the ladder to the steep shingle roof of the garage. Where she could see over the tree line, past the little dip to Green Arbor and out over the sparkling black-blue of Lake Michigan.

The lake was restless, patches of dark water churning against calm stretches. Only a few whitecaps between the two Lynx islands on the way to the shore, hidden by the town's buildings.

Past the town, past the Inn at the top of the first dune, out on its own little metal pier, the big square, red lighthouse stood patient and solid. A landmark that had guided ships past an odd shallow channel for more than a century before the Coast Guard declared it obsolete. Abandoned but not forgotten. Empty but not without purpose.

She remembered Graham's voice, unexpectedly animated during a historical society presentation last year. "The lighthouse wasn't just a warning system," he'd said, blue eyes bright with passion. "It was a promise. A reminder that someone was watching, waiting, making sure you found your way home." For a moment, she'd glimpsed the man beneath the careful exterior, and it had unsettled her in ways she still couldn't define.

"I'm not running away," she told the lighthouse across the distance. "I'm just... thinking about it."

But even as she said it, she knew she was lying. The metal had already decided. She needed to act. To do something.

She was going to apply for that position. She was going to stop chasing galleries in distant cities and see what happened when she stayed still long enough to be found.

In the distance, impossible but undeniable, the lighthouse beam flickered once in the morning sun. A broken bulb catching the light, probably. A trick of reflection on old glass.

She smoothed the wrinkled application on her thigh, already imagining her Dad's face—and Mrs. Frankl and Graham and all the rest—when they saw her name among the candidates. Would they be surprised? Pleased?

The thought made her stomach tighten in a way she wasn't ready to examine.

"Fine," she whispered to the universe, to the metal, to whatever part of Green Arbor's magic had decided to meddle in her life. "But I'm not giving tours in a period costume."

Chapter Two

Graham Cheever turned the first of three locks at six in the morning, a ritual as precise as morning prayer. The brass mechanism clicked with the satisfaction of well-maintained machinery, followed by the middle lock (installed after the break-in of '03) and finally the deadbolt (his own addition, because redundancy was just good sense). The bookstore door opened with a gentle chime that had announced arrivals since his grandfather's day, though at this hour, it only announced Graham's need for solitude.

Inside, Green Arbor Books exhaled its usual morning breath: old paper and binding glue, leather conditioner and yesterday's coffee. Today the vanilla ghost of Mrs. Frankl's afternoon tea. Graham inhaled deeply, letting the familiar cocktail settle his nerves. Here, in the geography of carefully alphabetized spines, the world made sense.

He moved through darkness with practiced ease, fingers finding light switches without conscious thought. The overhead fluorescents stayed off—harsh light was an assault on morning's delicate sensibilities. Instead, he clicked on the reading lamps one by one, creating pools of amber warmth between the stacks. The books seemed to stretch and yawn in the gentle illumination, gilt titles catching the light like sleepy eyes opening.

The coffee maker—industrial, reliable, definitely not magical—gurgled to life with its programmed precision. While it worked, Graham made his way to the back corner, to the Local History section that no one browsed before noon. Behind "Maritime Disasters of the Great Lakes" and "Indigenous Peoples of Northwest Michigan," a laptop waited in its hiding place.

Password: *StayingWasAChoice.*

He'd changed it from DadWouldUnderstand three months ago. Progress, his therapist would say, if he still saw a therapist. If he believed in progress rather than simply cataloging pain under different headings.

The manuscript opened to Chapter Eighteen, where protagonist Jake Morrison faced an impossible choice:

stay with his dying father or pursue the lead on a pair of nuclear missiles whose recovery could save thousands. Graham had been stuck on this scene for a week, the cursor blinking accusation with each passing second.

He started typing:

Jake stood in the hospital doorway, watching the machines breathe for the man who'd taught him to tie flies, to read river currents, to be still when the world demanded motion. His phone buzzed—intel from Sarajevo, time-sensitive, world-changing.

"Go," his father whispered, eyes still closed. "That's what I taught you to do. Go where you're needed."

But where was he needed most?

Five years, and the scene still hit too close to home. Graham's jaw clenched, fingers hesitating over the keys. The cursor blinked, patient and undemanding.

Graham closed the laptop. Some parallels were better left unwritten.

He removed his glasses, cleaned them with methodical precision. The morning ritual of transforming from Graham-who-writes to Graham-who-stays. That's what responsible people did.

The bell tower chimed eight o'clock, permission to begin the day properly. Graham returned his laptop to its hiding place, ensuring the false book spines aligned perfectly. "Secret Passages of Green Arbor"—even his deceptions maintained alphabetical order.

The bookstore revealed itself in daylight like a map of his psyche. The front section housed bestsellers and beach reads, commercial fiction that paid the bills and offended no sensibilities. These he arranged face-out, bright covers promising escape and happy endings. The middle kingdom held Literature with a capital L, properly alphabetized, some spine-out for the serious browsers who knew what they wanted.

But the back corners—those were his curatorial pride. Local history, land and lake. Maritime texts that Captain Bernie special-ordered. Poetry that seemed to rearrange itself nightly, rebellious verses refusing to stay ordered by author. And the section he'd never officially labeled but might as well mark "Katie Carter's Personal Library."

Welding techniques. Artist biographies. Creativity guides. Books on the intersection of craft and art, the philosophy of making, the spiritual dimension of working with fire. His latest acquisition, arrived yesterday, *The Metaphysics of Metal: Finding Truth in Transformation*. She'd mentioned it once, three months ago, lamenting its out-of-print status. Graham had spent two weeks tracking down a pristine copy from a dealer in Phoenix.

His fingers trembled slightly as he pulled the book from its shelf. The leather binding was cool under his touch, but his skin warmed as if absorbing some of

Katie's fire through the pages she would soon hold. He took a pen from his pocket and carefully wrote on the inside cover: "As requested - G." Simple. Understated. Nothing that would betray the hours he'd spent hunting for this particular volume.

His phone rested on the counter nearby. He reached for it, composing a text in his mind—*Found that book you mentioned. And the lighthouse manual came in yesterday*—then drew his hand back. Better to wait. Let her discover it herself.

She wouldn't notice. She never noticed the quiet accumulation of exactly what she needed.

Graham set the book aside and began his morning routine. Check the special orders (three romances for Betty Hartwell, a cookbook for the inn). Water the plants that thrived despite the bookstore's northern exposure and theoretical lack of photosynthesis-supporting light. Straighten the poetry section, which had somehow scrambled itself again—Dickinson mingling with Yeats, Oliver keeping company with Frost.

"Restless this morning?" he asked the stacks, then immediately categorized the question under Behaviors (subcategory: Concerning). Talking to books was one thing. Expecting them to answer was quite another.

The coffee maker beeped its completion. Graham poured a cup, added precisely one sugar (consistency in small things created stability in large ones), and settled behind the register to review his committee notes.

The lighthouse keeper position had been open for two weeks now. Applications would be accepted until the end of April, and Graham had been tasked with creating the evaluation criteria. He'd spent most of last night outlining what he felt were appropriate standards —historical knowledge, community engagement, practical maintenance skills.

At 2 AM, unable to sleep, he'd added a new section: "Artistic Merit." With subcategories for "portfolio evaluation" and "public engagement concepts." And a final addition, carefully worded to seem like standard boilerplate: "Demonstrated ability to utilize lighthouse studio space for artistic/creative endeavors with community benefit."

He stared at the page now, wondering if he'd been too obvious. The committee hadn't specified an artist for the position. But the lighthouse needed someone who could see beyond its history, who could bring it back to life. Who could transform it, the way Katie transformed metal into meaning.

The bell chimed at precisely nine AM. Mrs. Frankl entered bearing a bakery box and the expression of someone who'd appointed herself the universe's managing director.

"Graham." She met him at the square wood bookclub table tucked between Lit and poetry and set the box on its clean surface with deliberate care. "I trust you've prepared the criteria proposals."

"Color-coded by section." He produced the binders, each tabbed with military precision. "Historical requirements in blue, community engagement in green, practical skills in orange."

"And artistic considerations?" Her eyes held that gleam that preceded what she called "gentle suggestions" and everyone else called "orchestrated meddling."

"Purple section. Though I'm not sure artistic merit should be weighted as heavily as—"

"Nonsense. The lighthouse is a symbol, Graham. Symbols require artists to interpret them." She opened the bakery box, revealing pastries arranged with the same precision he brought to alphabetizing. "Besides, we both hope Katie applies. The deadline's not until month's end."

"Speculation."

"Observation. Liam mentioned Ella delivered the application yesterday." Mrs. Frankl selected a cheese danish, every movement deliberate. "Such a talented girl. Such passion. Shame she doesn't recognize care when it's right in front of her."

Graham busied himself arranging chairs. "I wouldn't presume to—"

"Of course not. You never presume. You simply stock exactly the books she needs, maintain a reference section that caters to her interests, and special order texts she mentions in passing." The gleam intensified. "Pure coincidence."

Before Graham could categorize an appropriate response, the door chimed again. Captain Bernie stumped in, followed by Dottie Kowalski and Art Haapala. Mayor Carter arrived last, his expression carefully neutral as he took his place at the table.

They arranged themselves around the table in the usual order: Mrs. Frankl at the "head," her back to poetry, Dottie and Art at her right, Captain Bernie in the wide chair with sturdy arms at the foot of the table, Mayor Carter and Graham with their backs to Literature. Graham closest to the cash register, door, and phone, although business on an early April Wednesday would not be brisk.

He spread the papers among them with bureaucratic precision. "As you can see, I've outlined the evaluation criteria we discussed last month. I've weighted historical knowledge at thirty percent, community engagement at twenty-five, practical maintenance at twenty, and artistic merit at twenty-five."

"Seems reasonable," Mayor Carter said, leafing through the pages. "Though I'd argue artistic merit could be higher. The lighthouse needs new life breathed into it."

Graham felt a flicker of surprise. "I assumed the historical society would prefer emphasis on preservation."

"Preservation doesn't mean stagnation," Mrs. Frankl said. "The lighthouse needs someone who sees its poetry, not just its history."

"Not everyone will agree—" Graham began.

The door burst open with enough force to rattle the window display. Katie Carter stood silhouetted in morning light, hair escaping from a messy bun like smoke seeking sky, wearing yesterday's welding clothes plus what appeared to be fresh coffee stains. April sunlight caught in her hair, turning ordinary brown to amber and copper, alive with possibility.

"Graham!" She moved through his carefully arranged store like a force of nature, leaving entropy in her wake. And God help him, he tracked every movement—the way she pushed hair from her face with the back of her wrist, how she bit her lower lip scanning shelves, the unconscious grace in hands that shaped metal and apparently his concentration into scrap. The familiar scent of her followed—metal and vanilla, impossibly combined, with something underneath that was purely Katie. His pulse jumped, his breathing shifting without permission.

"Please tell me you got that lighthouse manual in. And maybe 'Advanced Welding Techniques Volume Three'? The library's copy is missing pages and I need the section on—"

She stopped, finally noticing the committee arranged around the table. "Oh. Good morning, everyone." Her smile was warm before uncertainty shadowed it. "Sorry. Didn't realize you were having your lighthouse committee meeting."

"It's not secret," Graham said, already moving toward the special order shelf. "And you knew we met Wednesday mornings."

"I forgot what day it was." She followed him through the stacks, nervous energy radiating like heat from her skin. "Dad, hi. Mrs. Frankl. Everyone."

Graham's fingers found both books immediately— the welding text filed under C for Carter, though it belonged under W for Welding, and the lighthouse manual he'd special ordered last month. He'd been moving her books to their own section unconsciously, creating a Katie-shaped hole in his organizational system.

"Let me guess," she said, a smile playing at the corners of her mouth. "Already alphabetized your breakfast?"

"Let me guess," he countered, handing her the books. "Another midnight artistic crisis?"

"Three AM, actually." She took the lighthouse manual, surprise flickering across her face. "You actually found it? I mentioned this weeks ago."

"It came in yesterday." He cleared his throat. "Special order."

"You remembered." Something shifted in her expression, a brief softening before she clutched both books, defiance and exhaustion warring in her eyes. "Fifteen galleries, Graham. Fifteen rejections. Maybe I should face reality and do what you did. Choose responsibility over pipe dreams."

The committee had gone silent, watching them with the intensity of theater-goers at a particularly dramatic scene. Graham started to reach for her hand, then pulled back. He'd received his share of rejection letters—twenty-seven agent passes, four publisher declines. Each one filed away, never mentioned, never shared.

"Markets are subjective," he said, the words coming out stilted, insufficient.

"Right. Subjective." Her laugh had a bite. "What would steady, predictable Graham know about artistic frustration? You made your choice five years ago."

Direct hit. Graham felt it land somewhere between ribs, spreading like spilled ink. He filed the sensation under Wounds (subcategory: Deserved) and maintained his expression. But their eyes met and held for one breath, two, something flickering in the space between them before she looked away.

"Will that be all?" He gestured toward the register, professional distance restored.

"I think so." She looked down at the books in her hands. "How much do I owe you for the lighthouse manual?"

"It's on the house." The words escaped before he could reconsider them.

"Graham—"

"Professional courtesy. For the future lighthouse keeper." He risked a small smile.

"I haven't even applied yet."

"But you will."

Their fingers never quite touched as he handed her the books, but Graham was acutely aware of the small space between them, charged with something he couldn't name. Katie must have felt it too—she fumbled slightly, the welding manual slipping from her grasp and tumbling to the floor.

They both reached for it. Both stopped, gazes meeting for a suspended moment. The foot of space between them might as well have been a chasm.

"I've got it," she said quickly, her voice oddly breathless as she retrieved the book and clutched both volumes against her chest like armor. "Thanks."

The poetry section rustled ominously behind Mrs.

Frankl. The temperature in the store seemed to drop several degrees.

Katie paused at the door. "Good luck with your… criteria, or whatever." She glanced back at Graham, something unreadable in her expression. "Don't make it too complicated."

She left the way she'd come—chaos and coffee stains and the lingering scent of metal and morning. The door chimed closed behind her, leaving Graham to reconstruct his careful morning like a crime scene investigator.

"Well," Mayor Carter said into the silence. "That was—"

"Illuminating," Mrs. Frankl finished. "Graham, you were saying about the evaluation criteria?"

But Graham was watching through the window as Katie crossed the street, heading toward Carter Hardware around the corner, the lighthouse manual tucked securely under her arm. She'd left "The Metaphysics of Metal" on the counter, probably hadn't even seen his carefully printed note: "As requested - G."

"Graham?" Dottie prompted.

He turned back to the committee, filing his feelings under Later (subcategory: Always Later). "Yes. The evaluation criteria. As I was saying, I've weighted historical knowledge at thirty percent…"

The meeting proceeded with artificial normalcy, everyone pretending they hadn't just witnessed years of careful distance crack under the weight of fifteen rejections and one careless exchange. Graham took minutes with unnecessary precision, his handwriting growing smaller with each line.

When they finally dispersed an hour later, Mayor Carter lingered. "I hope she applies," he said quietly. "That lighthouse has been empty too long."

"The application deadline isn't until the end of the month," Graham replied, careful to keep his voice neutral. "She has time."

The mayor studied him with eyes that had watched Graham grow from angry teenager to careful man. "Maybe she needs someone to believe she's already what that lighthouse needs."

After everyone left, Graham returned his bookstore to order. Chairs precisely arranged. Coffee cups washed and dried. Katie's forgotten book moved to the hold shelf, labeled "Carter. Urgent." in his careful hand.

The poetry section had exploded in his absence— volumes scattered like birds startled into flight. Emily Dickinson lay open on the floor: "I dwell in Possibility —a fairer House than Prose."

Graham reshelved the books, but they felt restless under his hands. The whole store felt restless, as if Katie's brief presence had disturbed some careful equilibrium. Even the plants seemed to lean toward the door she'd exited.

His laptop called from its hiding place, Chapter Eighteen still waiting. Jake Morrison still frozen between duty and desire, between staying and going, between who he was and who he might become.

Graham made a note in his committee binder instead: "Review lighthouse keeper residential requirements." He paused, then added: "Professional artist workspace, northern exposure, industrial ventilation."

Because that's what responsible committee members did. They thought of practical improvements. They didn't imagine Katie Carter working by lighthouse light, sparks falling like stars into Lake Michigan. They didn't wonder what she'd create with steady income and dedicated space and someone who understood that rejection was just another word for "not yet."

His fingers hovered over the laptop's keys, then shifted to his phone instead. He composed a text, deleted it, rewrote it, deleted it again. Finally, the simplest version:

Lighthouse manual any help? Let me know if you need anything else.

He didn't send it. Not yet. Some things needed space to breathe, to transform. Like metal under heat.

The poetry section rustled again, pages turning without any draft to stir them. A book fell open to a passage highlighted by some previous reader: "The heart has many doors."

Graham closed the book carefully, placed it back on its shelf, and returned to his committee notes. The cursor blinked at the end of "industrial ventilation." He added: "and proper lighting for detail work."

Because maybe it was time to stop preparing and start hoping.

Chapter Three

Katie Carter changed shirts twice before settling on her original choice—ripped jeans, vintage Ozzy Osbourne tee, and absolutely no effort whatsoever. She wasn't dressing for Graham's visit. The fact that she'd even considered Ella's suggestion about the green shirt was just because it was clean, not because it "made her eyes pop" or whatever nonsense her sister-in-law had spouted.

She stomped out of the little log cabin that Liam had built for himself when he turned eighteen—no closets, ugh—and pulled up the garage door to her workroom. It wasn't cold, for April, but she was already overheating.

"This is about research, not impressing anyone," she told her reflection, yanking her hair into its usual messy bun. Her workshop mirror—salvaged from a Victorian dresser and now flecked with tiny metallic specks—reflected a woman who looked more uncertain than she wanted to admit.

The lighthouse application sat on her workbench, conspicuously blank except for her name and contact information. The morning light caught on the official city letterhead, making the page glow against the weathered wood. Katie turned away from it, focusing instead on the half-finished piece that had kept her up until three in the morning.

The metal—which probably used to be part of a truck, if the green paint she'd had to grind off was anything to go by—refused to cooperate. What had started as an abstract exploration of confinement now resembled—surprise—another lighthouse. This one more angular than her usual work, the twisted steel base rising into a silver column that caught the light like a beacon. Even when she tried to escape it, the lighthouse found her.

"Piece of junk," she muttered, pulling on her welding gloves. The leather was worn smooth in places, stiff with use in others, molded perfectly to her hands after years of work. The familiar weight was comforting, grounding her when everything else felt uncertain.

She fired up the torch, and the space around her started to fill with the odd garlicky scent of burning acetylene. The blue flame hissed and sputtered, hungry for work. Katie lowered her mask and leaned in, letting the heat push away all thoughts except shape and form.

Time dissolved in the rhythm of creation. The sizzle of metal, the weight of the torch in her hand, the dance of sparks against concrete floor. Outside, spring birds called to each other, their songs barely audible through the workshop walls and her focus. A bead of sweat traced her spine, tickling as it went, but she ignored it, lost in the piece taking shape before her.

But her ears were listening for the crunch of the driveway, and immediately yanked her back to reality.

Katie killed the torch with a sigh. Graham was early. She'd expected him after lunch, not at—she checked the old round clock on the wall—ten in the morning.

She yanked off her mask and gloves, wiping her hands on a shop rag that probably made them dirtier. He'd go around to the people-door on the side, even though the car-door was open. Probably didn't want to accidentally touch something hot, like she'd ever do that to him.

The knock, when it came, was precise—three evenly spaced taps, not too loud, not too soft. Exactly like the man himself.

"It's open," she called, turning on the shop fan. The rush of cool air felt good against her heated skin.

Graham backed in and then pivoted. The cardboard

box he carried looked heavy enough to strain even his tall frame. He wore his usual bookstore uniform: pressed khakis, button-down shirt with sleeves rolled to precise mid-forearm, and the reading glasses perched on his head that he never seemed to actually use. But there was something different today—a tension in his shoulders, a careful way he wasn't quite meeting her eyes.

"Morning." He set the box on a semi-cleared spot on her long workbench, keeping the wooden surface between them like a shield. "I brought those reference materials you might need. For the application." He gestured vaguely toward the half-completed form the box had pushed aside.

The scent of books—paper and binding glue and that indefinable smell of organization—mixed with the metal and ozone of the workshop. Katie wrinkled her nose slightly, the contrast between Graham's orderly world and her creative chaos suddenly sharp.

"That's a lot of books for one application," she said, moving closer to peer into the box. "What is this, the entire lighthouse section of your store?"

"Overstock," he said, too quickly. "The winter order came in duplicate. I thought you might make better use of them than the return shipping department."

She gave him a skeptical look. The books were too varied, too perfectly selected for her interests, to be random overstock. There was a comprehensive history of Michigan lighthouses, a technical manual on early 20th century lighting systems, a guide to maritime preservation techniques, and what looked like a coffee table book of lighthouse photography. At the bottom, almost hidden, a slim volume of poems about lighthouses and keepers.

"Quite a coincidence," she said dryly. "All these duplicates."

The edges of Graham's ears reddened slightly. He must have just had his dark hair cut. "Just good business sense. Better to distribute locally than pay return shipping."

"Right." Katie pulled out the technical manual. Graham had always been like this—helpful to a fault, finding exactly what everyone needed before they asked. Last month he'd left a book about pet care on Mrs. Mullaney's porch the day before her nephew arrived with an unexpected puppy. The year before, he'd somehow procured a rare gardening text for Captain Bernie two days before the man discovered Japanese beetles in his prize roses.

It was just Graham being Graham. Nothing special about him helping her.

"The lamp room restoration section is particularly useful," he said, nodding at the manual she'd selected. "Page ninety-four."

"You read it?" Katie raised an eyebrow.

"Skimmed it. Professional interest." He glanced around her workshop, gaze landing on her half-finished sculpture. "Another lighthouse?"

Heat crept up Katie's neck that had nothing to do with welding. "It's supposed to be abstract. Confinement and liberation. The metal had other ideas."

"It's beautiful." The words were simple, direct, without the qualifiers gallery directors always added. Beautiful but too regional. Beautiful but not innovative enough. Beautiful but not marketable.

"It's not finished," she countered, defensive out of habit.

"No," Graham agreed, his voice neutral. "But it knows what it wants to be."

Katie turned back to the box of books, not wanting to consider the meaning behind his words. "I haven't decided about applying," she said, though the lie felt obvious even to her. "It's a big commitment."

"Two years." Graham nodded. "Though the state said it could be extended if the keeper meets performance expectations."

"You've read the fine print."

"I read everything." His expression remained carefully pleasant. "It's an occupational hazard."

Katie sorted through the books, needing the distraction. "Thanks for these. I'll get them back to you—"

"Keep them." His voice was firm. "Consider it the bookstore's contribution to historic preservation."

"Graham—"

"Please." The word held something that made Katie look up sharply. For a brief moment, something flickered in his eyes—an intensity that surprised her—before it disappeared behind his usual careful expression. "You'd be good for the lighthouse."

She remembered, suddenly, watching him do this before. Junior year of high school, when Rick Sampson had asked her to prom. Graham had been tutoring her in calculus—ugh—and when Rick appeared with his awkward invitation, Graham had packed his books with the same measured movements, excused himself with the same careful smile, and disappeared.

Always stepping back. Always making space. It was what made Graham such a good friend. And sometimes drove her absolutely crazy.

"I don't know if I'm what they're looking for," she admitted, voicing the fear that had kept her from completing the application. "They probably want someone more... historically accurate. Someone who follows rules."

"They want someone who sees the lighthouse." Graham's tone was professional, like he was recommending a book to a customer. "Someone who understands that it's more than just a building."

"Like you?" The question slipped out before she could stop it.

"I understand buildings." He adjusted his glasses, one of his few nervous habits. "You understand transformation. What things can become."

There was a brief silence, awkward but not uncomfortable, before Graham cleared his throat and stepped back.

"I should get back to the store." His voice had returned to its careful neutrality.

"Right." Katie nodded, relieved to be back on familiar footing. "Thanks for the books."

"Of course." He was already at the door, retreating to safety. "Good luck with the application. If you decide."

After he left, Katie stood in her workshop, surrounded by the smell of acetylene, steel, and books, listening to his truck start and pull away. She shook her head slightly. Graham Cheever, town librarian and professional overthinker. Always trying to organize the world into neat categories, always slightly disappointed when it refused to comply.

Her phone buzzed. Liam.

Mom wants to know if you're coming to lunch. Dad has "thoughts" about the lighthouse position.

Katie sighed. Of course her father had thoughts. Everyone in Green Arbor seemed to have thoughts about what Katie Carter should do with her life. Everyone except Katie herself.

Be there at noon, she texted back, then looked at the application again. The blank spaces actually seemed less intimidating now, surrounded by Graham's carefully selected research materials.

She flipped open the technical manual to page ninety-four as he'd suggested. Someone—and she knew exactly who—had placed a bookmark there, a simple card with the bookstore's logo. On the back, in Graham's precise handwriting: *The light doesn't just guide ships home. It reminds them there's somewhere worth returning to.*

Typical Graham, finding the perfect quote for every situation. The man probably had a filing system for inspirational passages, organized by recipient and occasion. She slipped the bookmark into her pocket anyway. It was a good quote.

Katie cleaned up, changed shirts (into a clean blue one, not the green one Ella had suggested), and headed to the hardware store for lunch. She drove through town, past the turnoff to the boat launch, past the bookstore where Graham was visible through the window, carefully adjusting a display, and into the town parking lot.

Carter Hardware occupied the corner of Main and Lake, its brick facade weathered by decades of Michigan winters into something mellow and inviting. The family apartment took up the top floor, though her parents only used half of it now that she and Liam had moved out.

The smell hit her as soon as she entered—metal and oil and wood, underscored by the cinnamon of her mother's perpetual potpourri.

"There she is!" Her father's voice boomed from the back, where he was helping Stan Murphy select the right screws for whatever project he was terrorizing the town with this week. "My favorite daughter!"

"Your only daughter," Katie called back, like always. She made her way through aisles she could navigate blindfolded. The wooden floor creaked in the familiar places, welcoming her home.

"Doesn't make you any less my favorite." Dad finished with Stan and enveloped Katie in a hug that smelled of sawdust and the peppermints he kept in his pocket. His beard, more salt than pepper these days, tickled her forehead. "Your mother's upstairs with lunch. Go on up, I'll be there in five."

The apartment stairs were worn in the middle, shaped by generations of Carter feet. Katie ran her hand along the banister, feeling the smooth wood beneath her fingers, wondering how many times she'd made this climb. The apartment door stood open, releasing the scent of her mother's famous chicken salad and fresh bread.

"That better be my daughter," Mom called from the kitchen. "And she better be hungry!"

"Starving," Katie confirmed, following the voice and smell to the heart of the apartment. The kitchen was sunny and warm, windows open to the spring air, curtains dancing in the breeze. Her mother stood at the counter, hair pulled back in the same messy bun Katie had inherited, hands busy with lunch preparation.

"Perfect timing," Mom said, turning to kiss Katie's cheek. "Table's set. Grab the lemonade from the fridge?"

They moved around each other with the ease of long practice, setting up lunch on the small kitchen table that had hosted every important family discussion for thirty years. The familiar ritual settled something in Katie's chest, a restlessness she hadn't realized was there.

"So," Mom said as they sat, eyes too casual to be truly casual. "Liam mentioned you're considering the lighthouse position."

"I'm thinking about it," Katie admitted, spreading butter on warm bread. The taste, yeasty and rich, was like childhood. "It's a big decision."

"It's a good opportunity," Mom said, passing the chicken salad. "Steady income, health insurance, housing included. And that studio space on the first floor—it's perfect for your work."

"I know all the practical reasons," Katie sighed. "But it's two years, minimum. That's a long commitment."

"Longer than you planned to stay when you came back from Chicago?" Mom's question was gentle but direct.

"That was different. You were sick."

"And now I'm not." Mom reached across the table to squeeze Katie's hand. "And you're still here."

The words weren't accusatory, but Katie felt them like a weight nonetheless. Five years. Five years of temporary plans, of "just until" thinking. Five years of watching her classmates establish careers in Chicago and New York while she made garden sculptures for tourists.

"Would it be so terrible?" Mom asked. "Committing to stay?"

Before Katie could answer, Dad's heavy footsteps sounded on the stairs, and he appeared in the doorway, his smile broad beneath his beard.

"Smells amazing," he said, washing his hands at the sink. "What did I miss?"

"Just discussing Katie's lighthouse application," Mom said, passing him a plate.

"Ah." Dad sat heavily, his big frame making the chair creak. "Thinking of becoming a keeper, are you?"

"Thinking about it," Katie repeated, though the words felt less convincing each time.

"You know, your great-grandfather worked with the

man who built that lighthouse," Dad said, helping himself to chicken salad. "Carried stones up from the shore, mixed mortar in the dead of winter. Used to say it was the hardest job he ever loved."

"I didn't know that," Katie said, surprised. Family history was usually her mother's domain.

"Carter men have been building things in this town for generations," Dad continued. "Your brother builds with wood. I build with metal and tools. You build with fire and imagination. Different materials, same legacy."

"The lighthouse isn't just a job," Mom added. "It's a relationship with the town, with history."

"I know, I know," Katie said, trying not to sound defensive. "Graham gave me the same speech this morning. Along with half the lighthouse library."

Her parents exchanged a look.

"Graham brought you books?" Mom asked, too casually.

"'Overstock,'" Katie made air quotes. "About ten perfectly selected volumes that just happened to be duplicates."

Dad chuckled. "That boy hasn't changed since he was ten, has he? Always finding the exact right book for whoever needed it."

"He's not a boy, Dad. He's thirty-two."

"And still looking out for everyone in town," Mom said with a smile. "Remember when you twisted your ankle hiking and somehow he appeared with that wilderness first aid manual?"

"That's just Graham," Katie said dismissively. "He does that for everyone."

"Mmhmm." Mom's knowing hum was infuriating, even if Katie wasn't sure what she thought she knew.

"The point is," Dad said, "the lighthouse committee will be looking for someone who understands what that place means to Green Arbor. Not just a tour guide or a maintenance person. Someone who feels it."

"And you think that's me?" Katie asked, genuinely curious.

"I think that lighthouse has been calling your name since you were old enough to hold a crayon," Dad said. "How many drawings of it did you make? How many photos? How many metal sculptures that were 'abstract' but looked suspiciously like a certain tower on the point?"

Katie didn't have an answer for that. Her parents' home was filled with evidence—framed childhood drawings, high school photography projects, her first welded piece from college. All featuring the lighthouse in some form.

"Just think about it," Mom said. "Really think. Not about what you might miss somewhere else, but what you could build here."

After lunch, Katie helped clean up, the familiar

routine of washing while Mom dried as comforting as the meal itself. They worked in companionable silence, the only sounds the clink of dishes and the distant bell of the hardware store door as Dad helped customers downstairs. A month from now, they wouldn't be able to do this. Katie would be at the store nearly every day during summer season, so Dad and Mom could take a lunch break.

"He's proud of you, you know," Mom said eventually, putting away the last plate. "Whatever you decide."

"I know." Katie smiled, though it felt tight. "I just don't want to disappoint anyone."

"The only person you need to worry about disappointing is yourself," Mom said, wiping her hands on a towel. "The rest of us will be fine."

Katie hugged her mother goodbye, inhaling the scent of cinnamon and chicken salad and home, then headed back to her workshop. The afternoon sun cast long shadows across the gravel drive, and she could see dust motes dancing in the light through the windows as she approached.

Inside, everything was as she'd left it—the half-finished sculpture, the welding equipment, the box of books from Graham. And the application, still mostly blank, waiting for decisions.

Katie sat at her workbench and pulled the form toward her. The questions seemed less intimidating now, framed by her parents' confidence and Graham's practically provided research materials. She picked up a pen and began to write.

Why do you want to be the Green Arbor Lighthouse keeper?

The words came more easily than she expected, flowing from some place deep inside that had been waiting for this question. She wrote about growing up in the lighthouse's shadow, about metal and transformation, about guiding lights and finding home. About seeing the lighthouse not as a relic but as a living connection between past and future.

When she finished, the sun was setting, casting the workshop in amber light. Katie read over what she'd written, surprised by her own certainty. She wasn't promising forever—the position was two years, not eternity. But she was committing to something real, something rooted, something that acknowledged Green Arbor as more than just a temporary stopping place.

She signed her name at the bottom of the application, the pen scratching softly against paper in the quiet workshop. Outside, the evening birds had begun their chorus, a gentle backdrop to the moment of decision.

Her phone buzzed. Graham.

Just checking if the books were helpful.

Katie looked at the message, then at the application,

then at the sculpture that had known what it wanted to be all along.

Very. Application complete. Thanks for the push.

There was a long pause before his response came:

The lighthouse committee will be pleased to have a strong candidate.

So formal, so Graham. Katie rolled her eyes and texted back:

Any chance I could get more books if I get the position? That keeper's cottage has a lot of empty shelves.

His response came quickly: *Lighthouse keeper discount: 15% off. Poetry section: mandatory.*

Katie smiled despite herself. For all his careful distance, Graham could be funny when he relaxed enough to try. She set her phone down and turned to the sculpture, seeing now what it had been trying to become —not just a lighthouse, but a place of connection. A beacon calling not ships, but people. Home.

She picked up her torch again, the familiar weight an extension of her arm, her intention, her decision. The metal waited, patient and full of possibility. Ready to be transformed.

Ready to become what it was always meant to be.

Chapter Four

In the bookstore, Graham stared at his phone, at the message thread with Katie. His thumb hovered over the keyboard, where he'd typed and deleted three different responses before sending the safe, professional one about the committee being pleased.

When she'd followed up with that casual question about books for the lighthouse, something had loosened in his chest. He'd allowed himself the small joke about the poetry discount, a tiny glimpse of the person behind the careful facade.

Then he'd nearly followed it with something more—something about helping her move in, about building bookshelves to her specifications, about finally seeing her work with proper studio space. Words that crossed the careful boundary he'd maintained for years.

He deleted them all, of course. Just as he'd done that day in high school when Rick Sampson had asked her to prom. Just as he'd done when she dated Jason Collins during her brief return from art school. Just as he'd done every time she'd found another summer fling with some tourist who would never understand her the way—

Graham set his phone down and straightened the already-straight row of books on his desk. Then he opened his ordering software and began typing.

Advanced Lighthouse Maintenance: Modern Approaches to Historical Structures. Studio Lighting for Artists and Craftspeople. The Keeper's Library: Essential Maritime Reading.

Three books Katie would want, but probably wouldn't think to ask for. Three more books to add to the collection he'd been building for years, for someone who rarely noticed.

This time felt different, though. The lighthouse application wasn't just another art project or temporary job. It was a commitment to Green Arbor, to staying. To being found.

Graham closed his laptop. Some possibilities were better left unexplored. For now.

Two weeks later, Graham arrived at the bookstore at 5:30 AM to find poetry had staged a revolution.

Books lay scattered across the floor like broken birds, spines cracked open to their most painful verses. Emily Dickinson's complete works sprawled near the register, pages fluttering to "I had been hungry all the years." Neruda leaned against the wall, fallen open to "I love you without knowing how, or when, or from where." Every volume of unrequited love, every stanza of yearning, had apparently decided to free itself from alphabetical prison.

"Perfect." Graham set down his coffee—made wrong, too bitter, forgotten sugar like everything else he'd forgotten in the rush of committee preparation. The lighthouse application deadline had passed yesterday, and today the committee would begin their review. Including Katie's application, which he'd known was coming but still hadn't prepared himself to evaluate with professional distance.

He knelt among the poetry carnage, gathering volumes with hands that trembled slightly. Filed under: Exhaustion (subcategory: Emotional). Except his filing system seemed to be malfunctioning, because what he felt defied neat categorization. It sprawled messily across every careful boundary he'd built.

Byron joined the pile in his arms. "She walks in

beauty, like the night." Katie had worn green yesterday, dropping by to return a book. Sea glass, Ella had probably called it. Graham had noticed it made her eyes look like the lake before a storm.

The bookstore's temperature dropped a degree, breath misting in the early morning air. Even his sanctuary had opinions about his emotional state. The romance section rattled ominously from across the room, threatening its own rebellion.

"I'm handling it," Graham told the empty store. Then, because honesty seemed to be the morning's theme: "I'm categorically not handling it."

He finished collecting the poetry, reshelving with mechanical precision. Alphabetical by author, chronological within. Order from chaos. If only everything else could be so easily fixed.

Under his desk, the new *Michigan Review* sat hidden, his name one of the eight in tiny type on the cover. Another thing he'd never shown anyone. His laptop waited on top of the desk, but when he tried to open it, the password failed. *StayingWasAChoice* no longer worked. The cursor blinked mockingly.

Of course. Even his own technology knew he was a fraud.

Graham tried three variations before his fingers moved without conscious thought: *ChoosingToFight*.

The screen opened to Chapter Eighteen. Jake Morrison, still stuck between duty and desire, between staying safe and risking everything. He stared at the words for a long moment, then closed the file without reading further. Today required professional focus, not emotional indulgence.

He pulled the committee binder from his briefcase instead. Twenty-seven applications for the lighthouse keeper position, each one neatly organized with his evaluation rubric attached. Twenty-seven people who wanted to live in the keeper's cottage, maintain the historic structure, and serve as Green Arbor's maritime ambassador.

One application that mattered more than the others, though he couldn't let that show.

Graham sorted them into preliminary categories. Twelve clearly unqualified—people who romanticized lighthouse life without understanding the work involved. Eight with solid qualifications but no connection to the community or understanding of the lighthouse's significance. Five with promising backgrounds who might grow into the role.

And two exceptional candidates. Katie Carter and Eleanor Winters, a maritime historian from the University of Michigan with three books on Great Lakes lighthouses and a passion for preservation.

Graham set Katie's application aside for last, knowing he needed to read it with the same objective eye he'd given the others. Knowing he would fail at that entirely.

The bell tower chimed eight. Two hours until the committee meeting. Graham made a fresh pot of coffee, straightened shelves that didn't need straightening, and tried not to think about Katie's application waiting on his desk like a time bomb.

At 9:30, he finally surrendered to the inevitable and opened her file.

Her answer to "Why do you want to be the Green Arbor Lighthouse keeper?" made his breath catch.

The lighthouse has been calling me home since I was old enough to understand what home meant. I've watched its beam sweep across my childhood bedroom walls, heard its foghorn on stormy nights, traced its silhouette in countless drawings and sculptures. But it's more than familiarity—it's recognition.

Lighthouses and metalworkers share the same purpose: transformation. A lighthouse transforms darkness into guidance, danger into safety. Metal transforms under my torch from rigid to fluid to something new—something that carries meaning beyond its physical form.

I don't just see the lighthouse as a building to maintain or a tourist attraction to manage. I see it as a living connection between Green Arbor's past and future. My vision is to honor its historical significance while creating a space where community and creativity intersect.

The lighthouse has stood steady through generations of change, guiding ships to safe harbor. I want to guide people to understand that permanence and transformation aren't opposites—they're partners in creating something that lasts.

Graham closed the file, hands trembling slightly. Her words resonated with something deep inside him— the part that understood choosing to stay wasn't the same as being stuck. The part that had built a life around books and order while yearning for transformation.

He placed her application in the "exceptional" pile, writing careful notes on the evaluation form that emphasized her artistic vision, community connection, and practical metalworking skills that would benefit lighthouse maintenance. Nothing that showed his personal feelings. Nothing that revealed how her words had landed like stones in still water, ripples expanding outward.

At 9:55, Graham packed the applications into his briefcase, straightened his tie in the small mirror behind the counter, and locked the bookstore. The committee was meeting at the inn, neutral territory with the added benefit of Beatrice's cinnamon rolls.

The morning was cool for late April, spring still finding its footing in northern Michigan. Daffodils nodded along the sidewalk as Graham walked the three blocks and up the slope to the Starlight Arbor Inn, its weathered Victorian grandeur glowing in the morning light.

Inside, the committee had already gathered in the small conference room off the main parlor. Mayor Carter presided at the head of the table, with Mrs. Frankl and Captain Bernie to his right. Dottie Kowalski and Jim Hartwell from State Parks filled out the left side, leaving the foot of the table for Graham and his evaluation materials.

"Morning, Graham," Mayor Carter said as Graham distributed copies of his preliminary assessment. "You've been busy."

"Initial sorting by qualification," Graham said, maintaining his professional tone. "I've arranged them in four tiers for efficiency, but of course we'll review all applications."

"Twenty-seven," Mrs. Frankl mused, flipping through the top tier. "More interest than I expected for a position that requires living in an isolated cottage and giving tours to sunburned tourists."

"The lighthouse has a certain romance," Captain Bernie said, his weathered face creasing. "Until you've spent a winter there with the wind howling through every crack."

"That's why maintenance experience is heavily weighted in the evaluation criteria," Graham pointed out, opening his own binder. "Especially for candidates without local connections who might not understand Lake Michigan winters."

"Let's start with the top tier," Mayor Carter suggested, diplomatic as always. "You've identified three exceptional candidates?"

Graham nodded, carefully keeping his expression neutral. "Dr. Eleanor Winters from the University of Michigan. Maritime historian, published author, extensive experience with preservation projects. And Katie Carter, metal artist with demonstrated community connection and practical maintenance skills."

"Your daughter," Jim Hartwell said to the mayor, eyebrows raised.

"Which is why I'll be recusing myself from voting," Mayor Carter replied smoothly. "Though I'll participate in discussion as committee chair."

"Dr. Winters certainly has impressive credentials," Dottie remarked, scanning the application. "But no connection to Green Arbor specifically."

"Katie's application shows deep understanding of the lighthouse's significance to the community," Graham said, careful to use her first name as he would any candidate's. "Her artistic background would bring a unique perspective to programming."

"But does she have the historical knowledge?" Jim

asked, skeptical. "The state is especially concerned with historical accuracy in tours and educational materials."

"Her knowledge of local maritime history is well-documented," Captain Bernie interjected. "She's been picking my brain about lighthouse operations since she was twelve."

"And she's already outlined a partnership with the historical society in her proposal," Graham added, flipping to the relevant page. "Note the section on developing historically accurate interactive displays using traditional metalworking techniques."

Mrs. Frankl studied him over her reading glasses, something knowing in her expression. "You seem quite familiar with her application, Graham."

"I read all applications thoroughly," he replied, not meeting her eyes. "Dr. Winters also has compelling ideas about developing a research center focusing on Great Lakes maritime history."

"But would she stay?" Captain Bernie asked bluntly. "Academics tend to use these positions as stepping stones."

"The commitment is two years minimum," Jim reminded them. "Anyone could leave after that."

"True," Graham acknowledged, "but community integration increases retention rates. Dr. Winters would need to build those connections from scratch."

The discussion continued through the morning, the

committee methodically working through each application. Graham maintained his careful balance—acknowledging Katie's strengths without appearing to favor her, noting Dr. Winters' impressive qualifications without undermining her candidacy.

By noon, they had narrowed the field to five candidates for further consideration.

"I propose we conduct initial interviews via Zoom," Jim suggested. "Save travel expenses until we've narrowed to the final two or three."

"Agreed," Mayor Carter said. "We can schedule those for next week. Any objections?"

There were none. The committee moved on to scheduling details while Graham gathered his materials, relief washing through him. Katie had made the cut, legitimately and without any obvious advocacy on his part.

"The lighthouse manual you ordered was quite helpful," Mrs. Frankl murmured as they filed out of the conference room. "Katie mentioned it specifically in her application. Such a fortunate coincidence that you had it in stock."

Graham's ears warmed. "Just doing my job. Anticipating community needs."

"Mmm." Her knowing hum was infuriating. "And the advanced metalworking text she referenced? Another coincidence?"

"The bookstore serves all of Green Arbor," he said stiffly.

"Indeed it does." Mrs. Frankl patted his arm. "Some more... attentively than others."

The meeting adjourned, committee members dispersing into the bright spring day. Graham lingered on the inn's porch, watching Main Street's familiar rhythm of locals and early-season tourists. His phone felt heavy in his pocket, the message he needed to send like a stone he wasn't ready to lift.

Finally, he pulled it out and typed:

Lighthouse committee has reviewed all applications. Initial interviews will be conducted next week via Zoom. You'll receive official notification tomorrow, but I wanted to let you know your application was well-received.

Professional. Appropriate. Nothing that crossed the careful boundary he maintained.

His thumb hovered over the send button. Then, against better judgment, he added:

Your vision for the lighthouse was compelling. Good luck with the interview.

He pressed send before he could reconsider, then put his phone away and headed back to the bookstore. The poetry section would need reorganizing again—it always did after committee meetings. It was as if the books were responding to his emotional state.

Inside the store, he found the poetry perfectly

arranged—alphabetical, orderly, serene. But a single volume of Emily Dickinson lay open on his desk, the page marked with a lighthouse bookmark he didn't recognize.

"Hope is the thing with feathers That perches in the soul, And sings the tune without the words, And never stops at all."

Graham closed the book gently, returning it to its shelf. His laptop waited behind the false spines, the manuscript still open to Chapter Eighteen.

He sat down and began to type:

Jake Morrison had spent five years believing the lie that staying still was the same as being steady. That choosing safety was wisdom. That letting others make decisions was easier than fighting for what mattered.

He'd been wrong.

The mission would be dangerous. Probably foolish. But Jake was tired of watching from safe distances while others claimed what he'd been too afraid to reach for.

Time to choose differently.

The words flowed like water through a broken dam. The bookstore's temperature rose degree by degree, the chill of morning uncertainty replaced by afternoon purpose. Graham wrote until his fingers ached, until Jake Morrison broke free from the paralysis of indecision and chose a new path.

His phone buzzed. Katie.

Thanks for the heads up. And for the lighthouse manual. And all the other books I "happened" to need. You're a good friend, Graham.

Friend. The word sat like a stone. Safe, steady Graham. Background character in his own story.

He started to type the expected response—something pleasant and unrevealing—when a book fell from the shelf behind him. "The Art of War," landing open to a highlighted passage: "All warfare is based on deception. Hence, when we are able to attack, we must seem unable."

"Very subtle," Graham told his store.

Instead of the safe reply, he typed:

The committee would be lucky to have you. Green Arbor would be lucky to have you stay.

It wasn't a declaration. Wasn't crossing the careful boundary he'd maintained. But it was a small step away from safety, from filing himself under Friend (subcategory: Reliable).

His phone remained silent after that. Graham returned to his manuscript, to Jake Morrison choosing a different path, while the bookstore hummed quiet approval around him.

Because if Jake Morrison could choose to fight, so could Graham Cheever.

Even if he had no idea what that meant.

Chapter Five

Katie Carter stared at her laptop screen, watching her reflection distort as she moved closer then farther away. Was this how the committee would see her? Like some funhouse mirror version of herself, with bad lighting that turned her skin sallow and shadows that made her look like she hadn't slept in days?

"Come on," she muttered, adjusting the desk lamp for the seventh time. The Zoom interview was scheduled for tomorrow afternoon, and she still couldn't figure out how to look professional rather than panicked.

Her workshop wasn't exactly equipped for video conferencing. Metal sculptures cast strange shadows on the wall behind her. Tools hung in configurations that probably looked chaotic to anyone who didn't understand her system. The lighting was designed for welding, not broadcasting.

Katie groaned and slumped back in her chair. She didn't want to use a background—they always made her butterflying hands disappear. Inside the cottage was worse, dark and too close.

The chair creaked ominously, reminding her it was salvaged from the hardware store's back room and probably shouldn't be trusted with sudden movements. The smell of metal and machine oil permeated everything, a scent she normally found comforting but now worried might somehow transmit through the screen.

Her phone buzzed on the workbench. Ella.

How's the Zoom setup coming? Need any help?

Katie glanced at her laptop again. Her hair looked like she'd been electrocuted, and there was definitely a smudge of something dark on her cheek.

Disaster. I look like I'm filming a hostage video.

Three dots appeared, disappeared, then: *Ask Graham. He did all the virtual book clubs during lockdown. Lighting wizard.*

Katie's stomach did something complicated. Asking Graham felt like admitting defeat, like saying she couldn't handle this simple task on her own. But the alternative was showing up to her interview looking like she lived in a cave.

Doesn't he hate Zoom? I remember him complaining about it.

He perfected it anyway. Because Graham.

Because Graham. Two words that somehow explained everything. Because Graham would never let imperfect technology interfere with books reaching people. Because Graham would research the optimal lighting setup, the ideal background composition, the proper camera angle to reduce distortion.

Because Graham would know exactly how to make her look professional instead of panicked.

Katie's thumb hovered over his name on her contact list. When had asking Graham for help become so complicated? She'd been borrowing books, tools, and advice from him for years. This shouldn't feel different.

But it did.

Can you help me test my Zoom setup for the lighthouse interview? I'm a disaster.

She pressed send before she could overthink it further, then immediately regretted being so blunt. She should have eased into the request, asked how he was doing first, been less desperate-sounding.

His reply came almost immediately: *When?*

Now? If you're not busy?

Be there in 20

Katie looked around her workshop with fresh panic. It wasn't just the part of the space framed for a Zoom setup that was a disaster. The whole place reflected her chaotic week. Half-finished sculptures jutted from workbenches like metallic coral reefs. Reference books lay open, pages marked with peanut-butter-smudged sticky notes. Coffee mugs had multiplied in corners, abandoned in various states of emptiness.

She grabbed a trash bag and began shoving in the most obvious debris. The blessedly cool air flowing through the open garage door carried the scent of approaching rain, a welcome freshness. Outside, birds called to each other in the trees surrounding the property, their evening songs a gentle counterpoint to her frantic cleaning.

Eighteen minutes later (because Graham was never late), Katie had cleared enough space to make the workshop look intentionally artistic rather than criminally disorganized. She'd also made a half-hearted attempt to tame her hair and change into a shirt without obvious welding scars.

At the sound of a van pulling up, Katie wiped her suddenly damp palms on her jeans and took a deep breath. It's just Graham, she reminded herself. Predictable, reliable Graham who's helping with a technical problem. Nothing complicated.

His knock was precise as always—three evenly spaced taps that somehow conveyed both politeness and purpose. Katie opened the door to find him carrying what looked suspiciously like a professional lighting kit and a laptop bag.

"You came prepared," she said, stepping back to let him in.

"Zoom has specific requirements for optimal presentation." Graham's voice was matter-of-fact, but his eyes moved around her workshop with careful attention. He was wearing his usual khakis and a button-down, blue today, but something about him seemed different. More present, somehow. "Where's your setup?"

Katie gestured to the desk she'd cleared in the corner. "I tried using a lamp, but I either look like I'm in witness protection or auditioning for a horror movie."

The corner of Graham's mouth twitched, almost a smile. "Lighting is the most common mistake in video conferencing. That and camera angles." He set his equipment down and assessed the space, moving with unexpected efficiency. "May I?"

"Be my guest." Katie stood back. Graham pivoted her laptop screen toward the back instead of the side where she had it. He rearranged her workspace with the same methodical care he brought to alphabetizing books. His hands moved confidently, setting up a small light with a diffuser, positioning her laptop at a specific height, pulling her stool out from the shadows instead of the chair.

"The committee will be looking for confidence and

competence," he said, adjusting the small light. "You want to appear professional but approachable. Knowledgeable but not intimidating."

"That's a lot to convey through a computer screen."

"It's mostly about removing distractions." Graham stepped back to assess his work. "A clean background, good lighting, and comfortable positioning so you're not fidgeting or straining to see. And use earbuds."

Katie noticed he was carefully avoiding looking directly at her, focusing instead on the technical aspects of the setup. Maintaining professional distance, even here in her space. Made sense, but something about that bothered her.

"So," she said, filling the silence, "who else made the final cut? Am I up against museum curators or lighthouse enthusiasts?"

Graham's hands stilled momentarily. "The committee keeps candidate information confidential."

"Come on, Graham. It's me asking."

"Which is why I especially can't tell you." He looked up then, his expression carefully neutral. "It would be unethical to discuss other candidates."

Katie rolled her eyes. "Always by the book."

"The book exists for a reason." But there was no heat in his words, just that same steady certainty that used to drive her crazy and now just felt... familiar. Reliable.

"Fine. Don't tell me. I'll just assume I'm up against lighthouse experts with three PhDs and a Nobel Prize."

Graham made a small adjustment to her laptop screen. "You don't need to worry about other candidates. Your application was exceptional."

The simple statement, delivered without embellishment, made Katie's cheeks warm. Graham never offered empty compliments. If he said something was exceptional, he meant exactly that.

"Let's test the setup," he said, before she could respond. "I'll step outside and send you a link. Answer as if it's the actual interview."

Katie nodded, suddenly nervous again. Graham moved toward the door, then paused.

"One more thing." He reached into his bag and pulled out a book. "This might help. It has a section on the original lighthouse keeper's daily routine."

Katie took the book, their fingers not quite touching in the transfer. "More 'overstock?/"

Something that might have been a smile touched his eyes. "Pure coincidence."

Outside, rain had begun to fall, a gentle patter on the metal roof that filled the workshop with its comforting rhythm. Katie sat in her newly arranged chair, feeling oddly formal in her own space. The message popped up. She took a deep breath and clicked the link.

Graham appeared on her screen, sitting in his truck with the rain creating a soothing backdrop behind him. The contrast was striking—her in the warm, industrial space of her workshop, surrounded by metal and fire; him in the cool blue interior of his truck, rain blurring the world beyond his windows.

"Can you hear me clearly?" he asked, his voice coming through with surprising warmth despite the digital medium.

"Yes. Can you see me okay?"

"Sit up a bit. Yes." Graham adjusted something on his end. "Now, the committee will likely begin with standard questions about your qualifications and interest in the position. They'll be able to see you, but their view of your space will be limited to what appears behind you."

Katie glanced over her shoulder. The lighthouse sculpture she'd been working on was partly visible, its copper surface catching the light from Graham's setup.

"Is that okay? The sculpture?"

"Perfect," Graham said. "It shows what you do without being distracting."

They spent the next twenty minutes running through practice questions. Graham slipped effortlessly into the role of interviewer, asking about her vision for the lighthouse, her maintenance experience, her ideas for community engagement. His questions were thoughtful and specific, clearly designed to help her showcase her strengths.

"What about the studio space?" Katie asked during a pause. "Should I mention my plans for that?"

Graham considered this, his expression thoughtful. "Yes, but frame it as benefiting the community. The committee is looking for someone who sees the lighthouse as more than just a personal opportunity."

"It is more than that." Katie leaned forward, surprised by the intensity of her own feelings. "The lighthouse has been part of Green Arbor's identity for generations. It deserves someone who understands that."

Something shifted in Graham's expression, a softening around his eyes. "That's exactly what you should say tomorrow."

The rain had intensified, drumming on the roof and creating a cozy cocoon around their conversation.

"I think you're ready," Graham said finally. "Just be yourself, Katie. That's who they need."

The simple encouragement, delivered without qualification, made something catch in Katie's throat. "Thanks for this. I know you're busy."

"Never too busy to help a friend." Friend. The word hung between them, accurate but somehow insufficient.

They ended the call with awkward digital goodbyes, and moments later Katie heard Graham's truck door close outside. The rain had eased to a gentle mist, silvering the evening air as Graham walked back to her door.

"All set?" she asked, opening the door before he could knock.

"Everything's ready. Just don't move the laptop or lighting." He hesitated on the threshold, not quite entering, not quite leaving. "You'll do well tomorrow."

"Thanks to your help."

"No." Graham shook his head slightly. "You were always the right person for this position. The technology is just... formality."

Katie wanted to say something more, something that acknowledged the strange tension that seemed to hover between them lately. But Graham was already retreating, steps careful on the wet gravel, shoulders set in his typical squared posture.

"Graham," she called impulsively. He turned, rain misting his glasses slightly. "I'll let you know how it goes."

He nodded, the ghost of a smile touching his lips.

After he left, Katie sat in her workshop listening to the rain, surrounded by the setup Graham had created —practical, effective, thoughtful. Like him. She ran her fingers over the book he'd brought, this latest addition to his ongoing collection of "exactly what Katie needs before she knows she needs it."

When had she started noticing that?

The next afternoon found Katie perched in the same chair, wearing a dark blue top that Ella had insisted "brings out your eyes and looks professional on camera." Her hair was pulled back into something neater than her usual messy bun, and she'd even applied minimal makeup—enough to look polished but not so much that she felt like an imposter.

Two minutes before the scheduled interview, Katie's laptop chimed with an incoming text from Graham: *Remember to breathe.*

She smiled despite her nervousness. Trust Graham to know exactly what she needed to hear.

At precisely two o'clock, the Zoom room opened. The screen filled with the committee packed in the back half of the inn's dark wood conference table. Mrs. Frankl at the head, Captain Bernie and Dottie Kowalski to her right, Jim Hartwell and Mayor Carter to her left. And next to the mayor, Graham, his expression carefully professional.

The contrast between their environments was striking. The committee sat in the inn's warm, wood-paneled conference room, sunlight streaming through lace curtains behind them. Muted colors, soft edges, the occasional flicker of movement as Agnes or Beatrice passed by with coffee. The inn created an impression of history and continuity, stability and tradition.

Katie, meanwhile, sat surrounded by metal and tools, hard edges and industrial materials. Deep in the forest rather than on a sunny bluff looking out toward the lake.

"Good afternoon, Ms. Carter," Mrs. Frankl began, her voice crisp even through the digital connection. "Thank you for joining us today. We'll be asking several questions about your application for the lighthouse keeper position."

"I'm looking forward to it," Katie replied, consciously relaxing her shoulders the way Graham had suggested.

"Let's begin with your vision for the lighthouse," Mrs. Frankl continued. "In your application, you mentioned seeing it as a 'living connection between past and future.' Could you elaborate on what that means in practical terms?"

Katie took a breath, finding her rhythm. "The lighthouse has always served dual purposes—practical and symbolic. It guided ships safely through dangerous waters, but it also represented home, safety, and connection to those at sea. I see the modern lighthouse keeper's role similarly—maintaining the historic structure while helping people connect to its meaning in contemporary ways."

Captain Bernie went next. "And how would you handle the maintenance aspects? Lake Michigan winters can be brutal on the structure."

Katie smiled, warming to the subject. "I've been researching the original construction techniques and materials. My metalworking experience gives me an advantage in understanding structural integrity and weatherproofing. I'd implement preventative maintenance seasonally, focusing on the most vulnerable areas before winter storms hit."

As she spoke, Katie noticed Graham watching her with that careful attention he brought to everything. Not encouraging, not discouraging—just present, observing with those steady eyes that seemed to catalog every detail. Amazing how he could type notes into his laptop without ever looking at the keys.

The questions continued, each committee member taking turns. Jim Hartwell asked about tourist management, Dottie about educational programming, her dad the mayor about community integration. Katie answered each question thoughtfully, drawing on both her research and her personal connection to the lighthouse.

"And the studio space in the keeper's cottage," Mrs.

Frankl said finally. "How do you envision utilizing that area?"

Here was the question Graham had prepared her for. Katie glanced briefly at him before answering.

"The studio would serve multiple purposes," she said. "First, as a working artist's space where visitors could observe traditional metalworking techniques that connect to the lighthouse's original construction. Second, as a community resource for workshops and demonstrations. And third, as a creative laboratory for developing new educational displays for the lighthouse itself."

Mrs. Frankl's expression remained neutral, but Katie caught a slight nod from Graham—so subtle it was barely perceptible.

"One final question, Ms. Carter," Mrs. Frankl said. "Why should this committee select you over other quali-fied candidates?"

Katie paused, considering. She should say something about the history. Make connections.

"Because I understand both worlds," she said finally. "The practical and the symbolic. The historical signifi-cance and the future potential. The lighthouse isn't just a job to me—it's part of who I am and who Green Arbor is. I can honor its past while helping it evolve."

As she spoke, something subtle shifted in the inn's lighting—a warm glow that hadn't been there before, as if the building itself approved. Only Graham seemed to notice, his eyes flickering briefly to the wall behind Mrs. Frankl.

"I see," Mrs. Frankl said. "We appreciate your time and thoughtfulness. The committee will be conducting final interviews with all candidates this week, and we expect to make our decision by early next week."

"Thank you for the opportunity," Katie replied, maintaining her composure despite the flutter of nerves in her stomach. Her gaze met Graham's briefly before the call ended. His expression gave away nothing.

When the connection clicked off, Katie exhaled slowly, tension draining from her shoulders. Her jeans were soggy on the sides where she'd wiped her sweaty hands, again and again.

Had she done enough? Said the right things? Conveyed her passion without seeming desperate?

Her phone buzzed. Ella: *How did it go?*

How was she so fast? Of course, Ella the innkeeper would know exactly when the committee broke up.

Katie stared at the message, trying to formulate an answer. Before she could respond, another text arrived.

Graham: *Well done.*

Two simple words, but coming from Graham—who measured his praise as carefully as he measured coffee grounds—they meant everything. Katie found herself smiling at the screen, a warm feeling spreading through her chest.

Think it went well, she texted back to both of them. Then, to Graham only: *Thanks for your help. Couldn't have done it without you.*

His response came a moment later: *You absolutely could have. But I'm glad I could help.*

Katie set her phone down and looked around her workshop. The lighting Graham had set up cast everything in a soft glow that transformed ordinary tools into something almost magical.

For the first time since submitting her application, Katie allowed herself to truly imagine living there—waking up to lake views, working in the studio space, giving tours to visitors who might leave understanding why lighthouses mattered. It felt right in a way few things had since she'd returned to Green Arbor five years ago.

Her phone buzzed again. Mayor Carter, wearing his father hat rather than his committee hat: *Proud of you, kiddo. 'No matter what occurs!' haha*

Katie smiled. Whatever the committee decided, she had put herself out there for something she truly wanted. Not just another art show or gallery application—something rooted in Green Arbor, in home.

The realization settled over her with surprising weight. When had Green Arbor shifted from temporary refuge to potential future? When had staying become a choice rather than a concession?

The light from Graham's setup caught on her half-finished lighthouse.

Katie closed the laptop and reached for her mini-welder. She had a sculpture to finish.

Chapter Six

The Roastery glowed against the deepening twilight, its windows spilling warm light onto the sidewalk where potted flowers nodded in the brisk lake breeze. Inside, the air smelled of fresh coffee and cinnamon, underscored by the ever-present Green Arbor scent of lake water and pine that drifted through open windows. Conversations overlapped like waves against shore, punctuated by laughter and the occasional clink of glasses. And along the long table at the side of the main room, a celebration.

Graham took a deep breath before stepping in.

The Roastery occupied a restored 1920s brick building with gleaming original hardwood floors that seemed to hum beneath Graham's feet—though whether from the vibration of the vintage roasting machine at the back or something else entirely, he couldn't say. Copper pendant lights hung from exposed beam ceilings, casting pools of amber glow that made everyone look as though they'd been dipped in honey. The walls, painted a deep teal that mirrored the lake on clear days, were packed with local photography—familiar landscapes that somehow never looked quite the same twice.

At the center of it all was Katie, radiant with happiness, accepting congratulations from what appeared to be half the town. She must have come straight from her workshop—her jeans with a small burn mark on one thigh, a faded black t-shirt, hair escaping its messy bun—but something about her seemed transformed. More vivid, somehow. More present.

A scruffy queen, she sat in the middle of the café's centerpiece, a hand-carved maple communal table that ran along the east wall. Plates of those killer bite-sized vanilla cookies displayed like tribute on the table in front of her, and a big white ceramic mug of what Graham hoped was whipped cocoa. Or she'd be up all night.

Around the table sat her family, her friends, her clients. Her world.

On the other side of the room, behind the reclaimed elm counter, Ezra Van Sant orchestrated the evening with practiced ease, his movements like water finding its natural course as he and his sister Rosemary pulled espresso shots and steamed milk. The Roastery had been in their family for two generations, and locals swore Rosie could match a person to their perfect drink before they'd even opened their mouth to order.

The espresso machine hissed and sighed like a contented dragon, releasing aromatic steam that carried notes of chocolate, hazelnut, and something indefinable that reminded Graham of the moment just before dawn breaks over the lake. He accepted his usual americano, and headed to the back of the room.

At the back corner, a small stone fireplace crackled with flames that danced in impossible blues and greens when nobody was looking directly at them. Beside it, mismatched armchairs formed a semicircle. Nearby stood a bookshelf stocked with dog-eared paperbacks and a picture book titled *Lynx Legends of Northern Michigan*.

His spot. Graham let the rich bitterness of his americano roll across his tongue, carrying with it the earthy complexity that had made The Roastery famous beyond Michigan's borders.

"She looks happy," Ella said, materializing beside him with the innkeeper's gift for appearing exactly when needed. "You had something to do with that, I suspect."

Graham took a careful sip of coffee to avoid answering. "The committee made its decision based on qualifications," he said finally, keeping his voice neutral. "Katie earned her place as a finalist."

Ella's knowing smile suggested she heard what he wasn't saying. "Of course. Just like all those lighthouse books that appeared in your store by pure coincidence."

Across the room, Katie laughed at something her dad said, the sound rising above the general murmur of conversation. Graham found his attention drawn to her automatically, cataloging details with the precision that governed his life. The jaunty angle of her head when she was truly delighted, the way her hands moved as she spoke, the slight flush across her cheekbones from excitement and café warmth.

"Wonder who the other finalist is," Ella said. "Katie's been speculating all afternoon."

The question tightened something in Graham's chest. The weight of what he knew and couldn't share sat heavy between his ribs, making even the simple act of breathing feel complicated.

"The committee keeps candidate information confidential," he recited, the words practiced and hollow.

"Always by the book," Ella said, unconsciously echoing Katie's frequent observation. "Well, whoever it is, they'd better be prepared. Katie's all in."

Graham nodded, not trusting himself to speak. Across the room, Katie's attention had moved to a couple across the table from her, her animation undiminished as she described her vision for the lighthouse. He caught fragments of her words—"community connection" and "historical integrity" and "practical preservation"—all the elements that had made her application stand out to the committee.

All the elements that the other finalist had matched with his own compelling vision.

"Graham!" Katie's voice cut through his thoughts as she spotted him and waved him over. "Stop hiding in the corner. This is a celebration!"

He moved toward her automatically. The floor beneath his feet was slightly sticky from spilled drinks, the café's usual cleanliness compromised by the unexpected gathering. The scent of perfume and aftershave intensified as he passed through clusters of people, each distinct fragrance cataloged and assigned to its owner—Agnes's floral lavender, Captain Bernie's cedar and salt, Mrs. Frankl's subtle jasmine.

"There you are," Katie said when he reached her, her smile bright enough to power the lighthouse they were celebrating. Up close, he could smell the faint metallic tang that always clung to her clothes, mixed with vanilla and something uniquely Katie. "I was just telling everyone about the studio space in the keeper's cottage. Can you imagine having that much room to work? With that light?"

"It's an exceptional space," Graham agreed, careful to keep his tone professional despite the warmth spreading through his chest at her excitement. "North- and west-facing windows. Original hardwood floors."

"Windows I can open during the summer," Katie added, her eyes bright with plans. "Enough ventilation for proper metalwork without setting off smoke alarms. After Liam's garage, it'll be like working in a palace."

"You haven't seen the other finalist's application, have you?" Mrs. Mandaman asked, her teacher's curiosity evident. "Any hints about who you're up against?"

Graham felt rather than saw Katie turn toward him, felt the weight of her expectation.

"Probably some academic with three PhDs in maritime history," she said, still looking at him. "Someone who can recite lighthouse specifications in alphabetical order."

"Actually," Graham heard himself say, "Dr. Winters withdrew her application last week. The committee selected an artist as the second finalist."

He immediately regretted the words. Confidentiality had been his shield, his excuse for keeping Katie in the comfortable dark. Now he'd handed her a piece of information that would only lead to more questions.

"An artist?" Katie's eyes widened. "What kind of artist?"

Graham took a careful step back, physical distance to match his returning professional caution. "The committee—"

"—keeps candidate information confidential," Katie finished for him, rolling her eyes. "I know, I know. But you just told me they're an artist, so clearly there are some things you can share."

"That information was in the press release," Graham said, which was technically true—the release had mentioned "two artists with distinctive visions for the lighthouse's future."

Katie studied him for a moment, something calculating in her expression. "Fine. Keep your secrets, Graham Cheever. I'll find out soon enough."

The conversation moved on, and Graham returned to the safety of the wall and its dogeared paperbacks. But he remained aware of Katie watching him with new intensity, as if trying to decipher what else he might know. The café felt suddenly warmer, the air thicker.

Later, as the celebration began to wind down, Katie found him again, in one of the well-loved chairs beside the fireplace. The café had emptied somewhat, leaving pockets of quiet among the remaining conversations. She knelt down beside the arm of the chair, resting her hands on its corduroy padding. Graham's heart juttered painfully.

"Thank you," she said, her voice softer than before.

"For what?" Graham asked, genuinely puzzled.

"For everything these past two weeks." She smiled, the expression holding something he couldn't quite identify. "For being there."

The simple words settled somewhere beneath his ribs, warm and unexpected. Filed under: Gratitude (subcategory: Undeserved).

"Part of the job description," he said, the truth slipping out despite his better judgment. "Friend, supportive."

Katie's smile deepened, creating the small crease at the corner of her eyes that appeared only when her happiness was genuine. Another detail in Graham's growing catalog of Katie observations.

"Well, I should go. Got a lot to do this week. Before meeting my mysterious artist competition." She studied his face again, searching for clues he was determined not to provide. "Any last-minute advice from the all-knowing committee member?"

Graham weighed what he could say against what he should say. "Be yourself," he said finally. "Your vision for the lighthouse is compelling exactly as it is."

Katie's expression softened. "Thank you," she said again, this time barely above a whisper. She pushed herself up to standing, and turned away.

Graham's hand came up, as if to catch her.

And dropped, to land on the arm of the chair where her hands had just rested.

Katie left with Ella and Liam, turning once at the door to wave goodnight. Graham remained by the fireplace, watching the space where she had been, feeling the weight of what was coming press against his carefully maintained composure.

Chapter Seven

The following week passed in a blur of preparation. Katie had essentially moved into the bookstore's maritime section, surrounded by stacks of reference materials and notebooks filled with her distinctive handwriting. Graham found himself adjusting to her presence as if she'd always belonged there—moving differently through the shelves to accommodate her sprawled research, brewing coffee stronger than he preferred because she liked it that way, ordering additional lighthouse texts with the quiet certainty they would find their way to her corner.

"Listen to this," Katie said late Wednesday afternoon, looking up from a dusty volume about early Michigan lighthouses Graham had borrowed through inter-library loan. The afternoon light caught in her hair, turning ordinary brown to copper and gold. "The original Green Arbor keeper maintained flowering vines along the walkway to the lighthouse. How did they even survive?"

Graham glanced up from the inventory he was updating, allowing himself a moment to observe her—flushed with discovery, eyes bright with interest, one finger marking her place in the text while the other hand gestured animatedly.

"Nicholas Harmon," he said. "Keeper from 1889 to 1917. His logs are remarkably detailed about both lighthouse operations and his personal observations."

Katie stared at him. "How do you know that off the top of your head?"

"I read," Graham said simply, returning to his inventory. The truth—that he'd thoroughly reviewed all lighthouse materials while evaluating applications—would raise too many questions.

"You're weird, Graham Cheever," Katie said, but her tone held affection rather than criticism. "Weird and useful."

She returned to her research, and Graham returned to pretending he wasn't constantly aware of her presence, wasn't tracking the small sounds of pages turning and pen scratching against paper, wasn't noticing how the quality of light in his bookstore had somehow changed since she'd begun spending her days there.

By Friday, Katie had filled three of those artist's notebooks with observations, sketches, and plans. Graham watched her organize them with an unexpectedly methodical care. When he recognized his own influence in her newly developed color-coding system, a smile tugged at his lips.

"What?" she asked, catching him watching.

"Nothing," he said quickly. "Just noticing your organizational evolution."

Katie looked down at her neatly arranged materials, then back at him with a rueful smile. "Don't look so smug. It's purely practical."

"Of course."

"I'm serious! When I present to the committee, I need to find information quickly. It has nothing to do with your obsessive influence."

"Methodical," Graham corrected. "Not obsessive."

Katie laughed, the sound warming the late afternoon air. "Either way, your particular brand of order is apparently contagious."

Graham allowed himself a small smile, cataloging this moment under Unexpected Pleasures (subcategory: Katie Adopting His Systems).

"The evaluation begins Monday," he said, changing the subject to safer territory. "The committee has scheduled a welcome reception at the inn at ten."

"I know. Ella's been cleaning like the governor is

visiting." Katie closed her notebook, suddenly serious. "Graham, what if my vision isn't what they're looking for? What if this other artist has some revolutionary concept that makes mine look... provincial?"

The word choice—provincial—sent an unexpected chill through Graham. It was exactly the term Finn Davidson had used in his application to describe local artistic perceptions. The coincidence felt ominous.

"The committee selected you as a finalist because your vision has merit," he said. "Don't alter it to match what you think they want to hear."

Katie nodded, but uncertainty lingered in her expression. "I just keep thinking about the keeper's cottage. That studio space. What it would mean to have room to really work, to develop the ideas I've had backed up for years."

"It would mean a great deal," Graham agreed softly. The afternoon light had begun to fade, casting long shadows across the bookstore floor. Outside, Main Street was quiet, most shops closing for the day. Inside, time seemed suspended between moments, between what was and what might be.

"Well," Katie said finally, gathering her materials, "Gotta go. Hardware store's inventory is tomorrow, and then..." She grinned up at him. "Sunday is day for panic."

She paused at the door, hesitating as if there was

something more she wanted to say. "You'll be there Monday, right? As part of the committee?"

"I will."

"Good." Her smile returned, smaller but somehow more significant.

After she left, Graham stood in the center of his bookstore, surrounded by the familiar scents of paper and binding glue, the comforting sight of alphabetized spines, the quiet tick of the old clock above the register. Everything exactly as it had been before Katie had begun spending her days here.

Everything except, perhaps, himself.

Saturday morning found Graham at the inn for the final committee meeting before evaluations began. The conference room was filled with morning light, dust motes dancing in sunbeams that fell across the polished table. Through the open windows came the scent of early summer—freshly cut grass, blooming flowers, the ever-present lake breeze carrying hints of dune grass and water.

"Everything's ready," Mrs. Frankl was saying, her perfume mingling with the tea steam rising from her cup. "Both finalists will have equal access to the lighthouse and community resources. The evaluation period will last two weeks, with formal presentations to the committee on the final day."

Graham opened the evaluation packet before him, the paper cool and crisp beneath his fingers. Inside were the detailed schedules, rubrics, and materials for both finalists. His eyes moved automatically to the second name on the list—Finn Davidson, Mixed Media Artist, New York City.

The resume was impressive, exactly as Graham remembered from the application review. Graduate of Rhode Island School of Design. Residencies at prestigious institutions across the country. Works in respected collections. A rising star in the contemporary art world, bringing his considerable talents to Green Arbor's humble lighthouse.

"The accommodations are prepared?" Mayor Carter asked.

"Miss Carter will remain at her current residence," Mrs. Frankl replied. "Mr. Davidson will stay here for the duration of the evaluation."

The inn's heating system made a soft sound, almost like a hum of approval. Graham had noticed over the past year that the building seemed to have developed opinions nearly as strong as its resident innkeeper.

"I must say," Dottie Kowalski interjected, arranging her evaluation materials with a teacher's precision, "I'm quite excited about the possibilities. Both artists have such distinctive visions, yet I can see tremendous potential for collaboration."

Graham's hand tightened imperceptibly around his pen. "The position is for a single lighthouse keeper," he said, his voice carefully neutral despite the tension gathering at the base of his spine. "We should evaluate each candidate on their individual merits."

"Of course, of course," Mayor Carter agreed. "Though Dottie raises an interesting point about collaborative potential. Green Arbor has always valued community cooperation."

The discussion continued, but Graham found his attention drawn to the window, where he could just see the lighthouse in the distance—red against blue sky, solid and patient on its rocky point. The structure had stood for over a century, guiding ships safely through dangerous waters, a beacon calling people home.

Katie understood that—understood the lighthouse as more than just a venue for artistic expression or career advancement. She saw it as part of Green Arbor's heart, as essential to the town's identity as the lake itself.

Would the committee recognize that when comparing her vision to Finn Davidson's polished presentation? Would they see past the impressive resume to the fundamental difference in perspective?

"Graham? Your thoughts?" Mrs. Frankl's voice pulled him back to the meeting.

"I believe both candidates deserve equal consideration," he said, falling back on neutral committee-speak. "I look forward to seeing how their visions develop during the evaluation period."

The meeting concluded with final arrangements for Monday's welcome reception. Graham gathered his materials, the evaluation packet feeling heavier than its physical weight would suggest. Inside were the detailed criteria by which Katie's dream would be judged, alongside the credentials of someone who might take that dream from her.

And Graham could say nothing, warn her about nothing, do nothing but watch it unfold.

The professional distance he'd maintained for years —the careful boundary between committee member and friend, between public servant and private man— had never felt more like a prison.

Monday morning arrived with perfect early summer weather—clear blue sky, gentle breeze, temperature hovering at the ideal point between cool and warm. Graham stood in his bookstore at 5:30 AM, watching dawn break over Green Arbor with that special golden light that seemed reserved for significant days.

He'd been awake since four, sleep made impossible by thoughts that refused to be properly filed and categorized. Now he moved through his morning routine with distracted precision, taking comfort in the familiar rhythm of opening procedures. Three locks disengaged in sequence. Lights activated in specific order. Coffee measured to the exact gram.

The poetry section, he noticed, was perfectly arranged—books aligned with mathematical precision, alphabetized without a single volume out of place. Even the typically rebellious Dickinson collection stood in proper order, as if the books themselves recognized the importance of the day.

"Behaving yourselves for once?" Graham murmured, running a finger along the neat row of spines. "How suspicious."

He spent the next two hours reorganizing shelves that didn't need reorganizing, straightening displays that were already straight, checking inventory that had been verified the previous day. The physical activity helped quiet his mind, gave his hands something to do besides clench into fists whenever he thought about Finn Davidson's imminent arrival.

At precisely 8:47, the bell above the door announced Katie's arrival. She looked both determined and terrified, dressed in what Graham recognized as her version of professional attire—black jeans without rips, a dark green button-down that brought out her eyes, boots that had been actually polished rather than just wiped clean.

"You're early," he said, stating the obvious as a shield against all the things he couldn't say.

"Couldn't sleep," Katie replied, moving through the bookstore with the familiarity of someone who had spent countless hours there. "Figured I might as well face the day instead of staring at my ceiling."

Graham noticed the subtle signs of her nervousness —fingers tapping against her thigh, eyes moving too quickly around the room, the slight tension in her shoulders. He wanted to offer reassurance, but the words felt stuck somewhere between professional distance and personal concern.

"Coffee?" he offered instead.

"God, yes."

He poured her a cup, adding the precise amount of sugar she preferred, and set it on the counter between them. Katie wrapped her hands around the mug as if absorbing its warmth, the steam rising to cloud her face momentarily.

"I keep reminding myself it's just two weeks," she said after her first sip. "Two weeks of showing the committee why I'm the right person for this position."

"Two weeks of being exactly who you are," Graham

corrected gently. "That's what the committee needs to see."

"Yeah," Katie said, her voice whisper soft. "I just hope I'm enough."

The simple statement, filled with vulnerability he rarely witnessed in her, made something shift in Graham's chest. A tectonic movement of emotion he couldn't properly categorize.

"Katie," he said, her name feeling different in his mouth, weighted with all the things he couldn't express. "You are more than enough. Your vision for the lighthouse is exactly what Green Arbor needs."

She looked up again, surprise and something else flickering across her features. "That sounds suspiciously like inside information, Committee Member Cheever."

"Just an observation," Graham said, retreating to safer ground.

Katie smiled, some of the tension leaving her shoulders. "Well, thank you. For the coffee. For the pep talk. For..." She gestured vaguely around the bookstore. "Everything."

The moment stretched between them, filled with words neither seemed ready to say. Outside, Green Arbor was coming to life—shops opening, people moving along sidewalks, the town preparing for the day ahead. Inside, time seemed suspended, the bookstore a haven against whatever waited at the inn.

"I should go," Katie said finally, setting down her empty mug. "The reception starts at ten, but Ella wanted me there early so she could—what did she say?—make sure I was settled."

"Of course."

She moved toward the door, then paused, turning back with an expression Graham couldn't quite decipher. "See you there?"

"Of course."

Katie nodded, then surprised him by crossing back to the counter and placing her hand briefly over his. Her skin was warm from the coffee mug, slightly rough from metalwork. So, so familiar.

"For luck," she said, then withdrew her hand and was gone before Graham could process what had happened.

The bell above the door chimed her departure, the sound echoing in the suddenly empty bookstore. Graham stood motionless, looking down at his hand, feeling the ghost of her touch linger on his skin.

Outside, Green Arbor continued its morning rhythm—predictable, orderly, unchanged. Inside, something had shifted, as subtle as dust motes in sunlight, as profound as tides responding to moon pull.

Graham straightened his already-straight tie, checked his watch, and prepared to face the day ahead. Committee member. Bookstore owner. Observer. These were the roles he knew how to play, the boundaries he understood how to maintain.

Even if those boundaries had never felt more arbitrary, more like lines drawn in sand as the tide rolled in.

The lighthouse waited on its rocky point, patient and permanent. In two hours, Katie would meet Finn Davidson for the first time. And Graham would watch, silent and professional, as the future of the lighthouse—and perhaps more—began to take shape.

Filed under: Waiting (subcategory: Inevitable).

Chapter Eight

Katie Carter stood in the entry foyer of the Starlight Arbor Inn, absently tracing her finger along the edge of the massive sand globe that dominated the space. Inside the glass, golden particles swirled and settled, catching the morning light streaming through the leaded windows. The tiny replica of the lighthouse stood proud amidst miniature dunes, surrounded by what looked like glittering stars suspended in the liquid.

She hesitated, then placed her palm flat against the cool glass. The "sand" inside—finer than real sand, with flecks that caught the light like mica—began to swirl without her moving the globe, dancing in patterns that reminded her of metal under heat, fluid and alive with possibility.

"Well, that's new," Ella said, coming into the foyer from the innkeeper's apartment she now shared with her husband, Katie's older brother Liam. "Usually it just glows a little," she said. "I think the inn approves of you."

"Great. No pressure or anything." Katie wiped suddenly damp palms against her black jeans, wondering for the tenth time if she should have worn something more formal. Her dark green button-down and freshly polished boots had seemed professional enough in her workshop mirror, but now she wondered what a big-city "Capital A" Artist would consider appropriate for a professional evaluation.

The inn around her was a collage of texture and light —warm sage green walls with crisp white trim, polished wooden floors that creaked welcomingly underfoot, the scent of lemon polish and something baking wafting from deeper within. Morning sunlight streamed through the stained glass panels above the grand staircase, casting colored patterns across the entry. Everything glowed with care and history and that special warmth that seemed to pulse in the walls themselves.

"You're ready," Ella reminded her, straightening the collar of Katie's shirt with sisterly affection. "You earned this spot. Just be yourself."

Two weeks of being exactly who you are. Graham's words from that morning echoed in Katie's mind, along with the ghost sensation of her hand on his—a brief touch that had felt unexpectedly significant. She flexed her fingers, trying to dispel both the memory and the nerves crawling up her spine.

"How many people will be here?" Katie asked, moving toward the parlor where the reception would be held. The inn's front parlor opened to the left of the entry, a welcoming space of midnight blue velvet chairs and warm wooden tables arranged around a fieldstone fireplace. Above the mantle hung a painting of a lynx overlooking the dunes, its eyes seeming to follow her as she entered.

"Just the committee, a few Historical Society representatives, any random inn guest, and your competition," Ella answered, adjusting a vase of wildflowers on one of the side tables. "Plus me, of course. The inn insists on proper hospitality."

"The inn insists, huh?" Katie smiled despite her nerves. After nearly a year of Ella's management, everyone in Green Arbor spoke of the Starlight Arbor Inn as if it were a sentient being with opinions and preferences. Most dismissed it as whimsy, but Katie had spent enough time here to know better. The building had moods, preferences, and occasionally very firm ideas about who belonged where.

Right now, the inn felt expectant. The temperature was perfect, despite the cool wind coming off the lake she'd felt coming in. Here, soft breezes occasionally drifted through the semi-open windows, carrying the scent of pine and lake water.

"Do you know anything about the other finalist?" Katie asked, unable to help herself.

Ella's smile was too innocent to be trusted. "Only that he arrived late last night and the Rose Suite seems very pleased to have him as a guest."

"The Rose Suite has opinions on guests now?"

"The Rose Suite always has opinions. It's just usually more subtle about them." Ella checked her watch. "They'll be here soon. Want some tea to settle your nerves?"

Before Katie could answer, voices on the porch outside announced the committee's arrival. Her father wasn't coming; he'd recused himself after the finalists were announced. She recognized Dottie Kowalski's happy warble first, followed by Captain Bernie's deeper rumble. Then the voice she'd been straining to hear—Graham.

Katie smoothed her shirt one last time and straightened her shoulders. Her portfolio—a weathered leather case containing her lighthouse designs and photographs of her metalwork—felt suddenly heavy in her hands. Inside were weeks of preparation, years of dreaming, all focused on the lighthouse waiting on its rocky pier.

She stepped into the parlor, but stopped, unsure

where to sit. Or whether to sit, before the committee did. Or what to do with her hands, or her portfolio, or her life.

Finally, she remembered to breathe.

She stepped toward one of the sofas, and The committee members filed into the parlor, each nodding greetings. Coming from the dining-room side, Mrs. Frankl glowed in her signature lavender suit, while Jim Hartwell from State Parks looked Ranger-ready. Passing Katie in the foyer, Captain Bernie was already pulling at his tie, probably feeling strangled. Dottie Kowalski's yellow dress—and her smile at Katie—chirped as loud as she sometimes did.

And Graham—so different from the man who had made her coffee that morning. Here, he was Committee Member Cheever, in pressed slacks and a button-down that looked freshly ironed, his expression carefully professional as he took his place with the others.

Their eyes met briefly across the room, and something flickered in his—encouragement, perhaps, or concern—before his gaze returned to careful neutrality.

The committee members all chose chairs, leaving the matching blue velvet sofa for Katie.

She was trying to get her legs to move toward the sofa when Mrs. Frankl spoke.

"Miss Carter, thank you for joining us," Mrs. Frankl

began, settling deeper into her chair. "We're just waiting for—ah, here he is."

The inn's front door opened, the distinctive chime announcing a new arrival. Katie turned toward the sound and felt the air shift around her—not just from the breeze that swept in from outside, but from something changing in the room's energy.

The man who entered looked like he'd stepped out of an artist's studio in a glossy magazine. Tall and lean, with dark hair tousled in a way that somehow looked both effortless and precisely arranged. He wore clothes that managed to appear both comfortable and expensive —dark slacks without a single paint smudge, a tan button-down with the sleeves rolled up far enough to reveal forearms marked with a few artistic tattoos, leather shoes that had probably cost more than Katie's annual art-supply budget.

But it was his face that caught and held her attention. Strong features softened by an artist's observant eyes, the kind that seemed to take in everything at once. Those eyes found hers immediately, widening with what looked like genuine recognition.

"Katie Carter," he said, crossing the room with confident strides, hand extended. "Your metalwork series about transformation is remarkable. The way you manipulated the copper in your Interlochen memorial piece—I've never seen anything like it."

Katie shook his hand on autopilot, momentarily speechless. He knew her work. Not just recognized her name, but actually knew specific pieces she'd created.

"Thank you," she managed, finding her voice. "And you're..."

"Finn Davidson." His smile was warm and direct. "Mixed media, primarily ceramics and installation work. It's an honor to compete with an artist of your caliber."

The committee watched their exchange with obvious pleasure. Katie caught Mrs. Frankl and Dottie exchanging satisfied glances, while Jim Hartwell nodded approvingly. Only Graham stayed cool, though Katie thought she detected a slight tension in his jaw.

Mrs. Frankl introduced Finn around. He had a kind word or reference to that person's questions during the zoom interview for every person. Even Graham warmed to Finn's reference to how organized the whole experience had been.

"Well!" Mrs. Frankl clapped her hands once, gathering attention. "Now that introductions are made, let's begin. We'll start with a review of portfolios here at the inn, followed by lunch, then proceed to the lighthouse for the afternoon tour."

The next hour passed in a blur. Finn sat on the other edge of the sofa, a full seat cushion between them. Which was good, because they both were hand-wavers. He waved her to start her presentation first, but at least didn't say something dumb like "ladies first."

Katie tugged the coffee table in front of them to her side, opened up her portfolio and propped it on the table at an angle that everyone, including Finn could see it. And, somehow, she got started, showing pages of current work and possible future work featuring the lighthouse.

The committee's questions were thoughtful and specific, focusing on her vision for community engagement and historical preservation. Katie answered with growing confidence, her initial nervousness fading as she spoke about the lighthouse she'd loved since childhood.

But it was Finn's reaction that surprised her most. As she described her ideas for interactive metalwork displays showcasing the lighthouse's original construction techniques, he leaned forward with genuine interest.

"You've created a new welding technique here," he said, pointing to a photograph of her most recent sculpture. "The way you've manipulated the metal to catch light from multiple angles—I've never seen that approach before."

"It's something I've been developing," Katie admitted, pleased and slightly disarmed. "Traditional techniques weren't giving me the effect I wanted, so I started experimenting."

"That's exactly the kind of innovation that keeps traditional crafts alive," Finn said, his enthusiasm seemingly genuine. "Taking historical methods and pushing them forward."

When Finn presented his own portfolio, Katie was equally impressed. His ceramic work was sophisticated and thoughtful, incorporating elements of the landscapes—both city and beachside—where he worked. His vision for the lighthouse included community workshops and rotating exhibitions featuring local artists alongside national names.

"I believe lighthouses were always about connection," Finn said, his hands moving expressively as he spoke. "Connecting ship to shore, danger to safety, isolation to community. That's what I want to capture in this project—connection across different media, different perspectives, different artistic traditions."

It was a compelling vision. Katie found herself nodding along with the committee members, seeing the possibilities in what he described. When their eyes met after she'd asked a methods question, there was a moment of professional recognition—one artist acknowledging another's skill and vision.

Graham was unusually quiet.

The morning session concluded, and the committee announced a brief lunch break before the lighthouse tour. Katie gathered her materials, hyperaware of

Graham helping Mrs. Frankl with her papers, his movements precise and careful, his expression still professionally unreadable.

"That went well," Finn said as Katie closed her portfolio. "Your connection to this place really comes through in your work. It's authentic."

"Thanks," Katie replied, surprised by the compliment. "Your installations are incredible. I especially liked the ceramic wave forms you did for that coastal museum."

"The Monterey project." Finn smiled. "Similar challenges to what we'd face here, actually—marrying contemporary art with historical architecture while honoring the location's purpose."

"We?" Katie caught the pronoun choice.

"Force of habit." Finn's smile turned slightly self-deprecating. "I tend to think collaboratively. Hard to turn off." Before Katie could respond, Ella appeared to announce lunch was ready in the dining room.

The meal passed pleasantly enough—simple sandwiches and salads that showcased local ingredients, especially cherries and cranberries, served on the inn's blue willow china. Katie was seated between Captain Bernie and Finn, the conversation flowing easily between lighthouse history and artistic approaches.

Throughout the meal, she was aware of Graham at the far end of the table, contributing only occasionally to the discussion. Once, their eyes met across the plates and glasses, and Katie thought she saw something unspoken in his gaze—a question, perhaps, or a warning. But then Finn asked her opinion on community workshops, and the moment passed.

After lunch, they gathered in the inn's front yard to walk to the lighthouse. The day had warmed to perfect early summer weather, sunshine tempered by a cool breeze off the lake. The path to the lighthouse wound past pine trees and dune grass, the scent of warming sand and evergreen filling the air.

Katie fell into step beside Finn, with the committee members following behind. The gravel crunched pleasantly beneath her boots, a sound that had accompanied countless walks to the lighthouse throughout her life. But today felt different—today she walked the path not just as a visitor or admirer, but as someone who might become the lighthouse's keeper.

"The sightlines from town to lighthouse are so intentional," Finn observed, gesturing toward the red structure growing larger as they approached. "Like a visual conversation between structures."

"Exactly," Katie agreed, surprised he'd noticed the same architectural relationship she'd always appreciated. "The original builders positioned it to be visible from specific points in town—the inn, the harbor, the main street crossroads."

"Navigation isn't just for ships," Finn said, nodding. "It's for the people who stay on shore too."

The observation struck Katie as unexpectedly insightful. She glanced back, finding Graham walking several paces behind with Mrs. Frankl, his expression closed even as the heat of exertion brought a slight flush to his face.

As they neared the big red lighthouse, its square of faded walls glowing in the sun, Katie felt the familiar tightening in her throat—the emotional response she'd had to this structure since childhood. Big Red was the color of fresh blood, of forge-heated metal just before it became malleable, of every rejection letter's letterhead burned in her backyard. That square tower didn't just stand on its pier—it claimed it, possessed it, dared the lake to try something.

"It's beautiful," Finn said quietly, and Katie heard genuine appreciation in his voice. "Photographs don't capture its presence."

"No," she agreed. "They never do."

The limestone pier was a runway, a bridge, a 1,100-foot excuse to walk away from shore and all its complications. She loved how the waves crashed against it in storms, sending spray up and over anyone brave enough to walk its length. The lighthouse's industrial bones called to her—all that steel and iron, the rivets like jewelry, the way the upper gallery railing had been wrought by hands that understood metal's stubbornness and its willingness to yield if you just applied the right heat, the right pressure.

Captain Bernie passed them to unlock the lighthouse door, and soon they were stepping into the cool interior. The sudden temperature change raised goosebumps on Katie's arms as she moved from bright sunshine into the stone entryway. The smell hit her immediately—stone and metal and history, with undertones of lake air and old wood.

"The original structure was built in 1871," Captain Bernie said, his voice echoing slightly in the nearly empty space. "What you're seeing now includes renovations from 1924 and some restoration work from the 1980s."

Katie already knew the history by heart, but she listened attentively as the tour continued, watching Finn's reactions as much as the lighthouse itself. He asked smart questions about structural elements and preservation techniques, showing genuine interest in the building's history and function.

The narrow spiral staircase led them upward, footsteps echoing against metal steps, hands sliding along the cool railing. Katie felt the pounding of her chest as they climbed—partly from exertion, partly from the emotion of ascending toward the heart of the lighthouse. Sunlight streamed through small windows at regular intervals, creating dramatic shadows that shifted as they moved.

When they reached the lamp room at the top, the view stole her breath. It always did. Lake Michigan stretched endlessly before them, a vast expanse of blue meeting blue at the horizon. To the north, Green Arbor nestled against the shoreline, its buildings tiny from this height.

"Feels like you could see forever," Finn murmured, moving to stand beside her at the windows. "Like you're suspended between earth and sky."

The words captured exactly what Katie had always felt but never quite articulated. She glanced at him with new appreciation, a kindred soul.

"That's why lighthouses matter," she said. "They're thresholds between elements, between states of being. Safety and danger. Land and water. Known and unknown."

Finn nodded. "Liminal spaces. That's what makes them so powerful as symbols."

From across the lamp room, Katie caught Graham watching them intently. When he met her gaze, he looked away, examining the old lamp's mechanism.

When that light blazed—because it did blaze, not sweep, not shine, but blazed—it turned the water into hammered copper, into possibilities, into a canvas of light and shadow that made her fingers itch for her welding torch. She wanted to make art that captured that transformation, that moment when function became beauty without trying.

The other committee members moved around the space, making notes and discussing technical details, while Katie remained by the window facing the town, absorbing the view she hoped would become part of her daily life.

The keeper's cottage came next, tucked into the forest at the edge of the lake. The cottage itself looked tired, needed work—cedar shingles curling like dried leaves, windows that probably rattled in storms. But that was just surface. The bones were good. She could tell from the foundation stones, from the way the roofline held true despite decades of Michigan winters. Katie had only been inside once before, during a historical tour years ago. Her heart started to hammer as Captain Bernie unlocked the door.

The cottage was small but bigger than Liam's cottage, and with closets, at least. The rooms that had housed generations of keepers and their families had solid double-paned windows and almost no furniture. Original dark hardwood floors creaked beneath their feet as they moved through the living quarters, familiar and warm.

But the cottage wasn't where she'd really work. Not in some converted bedroom but in what the plans called a "workshop addition" that some previous keeper had built. Southern exposure through windows that went floor to ceiling, concrete floors that could take the abuse of dropped metal and slag, electrical that could handle a welder, a forge, whatever she needed.

"The ventilation system was updated last year," Jim Hartwell explained, pointing to vents along the walls. "Get it up to code for habitation, but more than that. Specifically designed to accommodate artistic work that might generate fumes or require air circulation."

Katie could already see it—her welding equipment arranged along the east wall, workbenches beneath the windows, finished pieces displayed on the northern side where visitors could view them during open studio hours. The space was larger than Liam's garage—almost a two-car garage—with better light and ventilation. The steady purr of lake waves through the windows would provide the perfect working soundtrack.

She turned instinctively, seeking Graham's eyes across the room, wanting to share her excitement with the person who had listened to her dreams for weeks. But he'd lagged behind, still somewhere in the cottage.

Then Finn was beside her, his hand light on her shoulder as he directed her attention to a feature she hadn't noticed.

"Look at the light quality on this wall," he said, gesturing to the northwest corner. "Perfect for displaying metal pieces. The way it would catch your surface treatments—those pieces would glow."

"Of course, this space would be ideal for our collaborative vision," Finn continued, seemingly oblivious to the temperature change. "Your metalwork and my ceramic pieces in conversation with each other, showing visitors how different media can interpret the same themes."

Our collaborative vision. The phrase caught Katie by surprise. When had they discussed collaboration?

The room's temperature dropped so suddenly that Katie's breath misted for just a moment—there and gone before she could be certain. The afternoon light through the windows dimmed as if a cloud had passed, though the June sky remained stubbornly clear.

Graham shifted, his jacket rustling in the sudden stillness. "The cottage gets drafts," he said, but his eyes moved to the windows with something like recognition.

The tour concluded with a walk around the lighthouse grounds, discussing maintenance needs and public access considerations. By the time they returned to the inn in late afternoon, Katie's mind was whirling with impressions, ideas, and questions.

"The committee will meet briefly to discuss today's observations," Mrs. Frankl said as they gathered once more in the inn's parlor. "Tomorrow begins your individual evaluation activities. Katie, you'll start with a community engagement session at the historical society at eleven. Finn, you'll begin with a maintenance assessment at the lighthouse at the same time. You'll find detailed schedules in your information packets."

After final instructions and a few more questions, the committee members departed, leaving Katie and Finn in the inn's parlor. Ella came in, carrying a tray that held both teapot and a bottle of Leelanau wine.

"Tea? Or something stronger after a long day?" she offered.

"Tea," Katie said."

"Yes, tea would be perfect, thank you," Finn answered with a smile that Katie noticed made Ella blush slightly. The man had charisma, no question about it.

As Ella poured their drinks, Katie sank into one of the chairs. Finn Davidson was not at all what she had expected. Not one of those pretentious New York artists, but someone genuinely talented who seemed to appreciate her work and Green Arbor's unique character. His vision for the lighthouse was thoughtful and compelling, with many elements that resonated with her own ideas.

Yet something felt off—a subtle dissonance she couldn't quite identify. Perhaps it was just the natural tension of competition, or the strange experience of having her artistic vision evaluated so formally.

"To new beginnings," Finn said, raising his teacup in a small toast. "And two weeks of showing Green Arbor what artists can do for a lighthouse."

Katie returned the toast, the lemony tea warming her from inside as the late-afternoon sunlight slanted through the inn's windows, turning the parlor golden. Outside, she could just see the lighthouse in the distance, solid and patient on its rocky point.

"It was a good first day," Finn continued. "I'd love to discuss some ideas over dinner—or breakfast tomorrow, if you're free before your historical society session. I think there are some fascinating possibilities for collaboration between our approaches."

Before Katie could respond, her phone vibrated in her pocket. She pulled it out to find a text from Graham: *How did it go?*

So simple, just three words, yet they sent an unexpected warmth through her chest. He'd been so distant all day.

"I should probably head home," Katie said, putting her phone away without responding yet. "It's been a long day, my head is so full! And tomorrow will be busy."

"Of course." Finn's smile was understanding. "Rain check on breakfast? Perhaps later in the week?"

Katie nodded, gathering her portfolio and saying her goodbyes. The drive home was peaceful in the evening light, Green Arbor settling into its summer rhythm around her. With the windows on her 1967 Ford rolled down, she caught birds calling from the trees, the scent of grilling food from the first of the backyard barbecues, and, always, the taste of Lake Michigan.

Back in her workshop, surrounded by the familiar scent of metal and possibility, Katie finally allowed herself to fully process the day. She set her portfolio on the workbench, grabbed a soda out of the minifridge by the door, and stared at the half-finished lighthouse sculpture she'd been working on for weeks.

Finn's artistic vision was compelling, sophisticated, informed by experiences she'd never had. His ideas for the lighthouse would certainly bring attention to Green Arbor, would elevate the site beyond local significance. There was genuine merit in his approach, and she couldn't deny the professional respect she felt for his work.

Yet her own vision—rooted in this place, in metal and fire and history—felt equally valid, equally important. Perhaps less sophisticated in some ways, but authentic in ways that mattered.

Her phone buzzed with a text from unknown: *Hey, it's Finn. Would love your thoughts on collaborative possibilities. Breakfast tomorrow? I have some ideas that might interest you.*

Katie stared at the message, feeling both flattered by

his professional interest and wary of what "collaborative possibilities" might mean for her individual vision. And how did he get her number?

Before she could decide how to respond, she saw the earlier text, from Graham.

She responded to Graham first: *Day one down. This is really happening.*

His reply came quickly: *You were impressive today.*

The compliment, so straightforward and unembellished, warmed her more than Finn's sophisticated praise had. Graham had seen her in the lighthouse space, had watched her reaction to the studio, had understood what it meant to her without her saying a word.

Katie picked up her torch, the familiar weight centering her as she prepared to work on her sculpture. Tomorrow would bring new challenges, new evaluations, new opportunities to show the committee her vision for the lighthouse. But tonight, she would lose herself in metal and fire, in the work that had always been her truest voice.

Before she adjusted her mask and lit the torch, Katie sent a response to Finn: *Breakfast tomorrow sounds great.*

Chapter Nine

Tuesday morning arrived with lake fog so thick Katie could barely see the Inn's front porch from the parking area. The moisture beaded on her truck's windshield like a thousand tiny lenses, each one reflecting the warm glow spilling from the Starlight Arbor's windows. She sat for a moment, engine ticking as it cooled, trying to calm the flutter in her stomach.

Just breakfast. With another artist. A professional meeting between two finalists.

Who was she kidding?

The Inn's front door opened before she could knock, Mrs. Frankl appearing with a knowing smile that made Katie want to turn around and drive home.

"He's in the dining room," Mrs. Frankl said, taking

Katie's jacket. "Asked specifically for the table by the bay window."

The dining room.

Katie stepped through the French doors and her chest tightened with memory. Six months ago, these dark wood tables had held centerpieces of wildflowers and copper wire sculptures she'd made specially for the occasion. Ella in her grandmother's wedding dress, Liam looking like someone had hit him with a happiness stick. The blue willow china—the Inn's original set, Ella had told her with reverence—catching candlelight as toasts were raised. Tom's breathless best man speech after his race from DC, everyone laughing as he talked about knowing from seven hundred miles away that his brother was "completely gone" for Ella.

Now morning light streamed through those tall windows, their small divided panes fracturing sunshine into geometric patterns across the polished floor. The botanical prints on the cream walls looked fresh as spring itself—Michigan wildflowers rendered in loving detail, probably by some long-ago artist who'd understood that trilliums were more than just plants. They were promises that spring would come again.

The mahogany sideboard gleamed with the kind of polish that came from daily attention, not neglect and sudden panic. Agnes or Beatrice must oil it every morning, the way some people said prayers. Above it, that moody oil painting of the Inn in its early days. Someone had captured not just the building but its soul—patient, enduring, slightly smug.

The tables were scattered with what looked like accident but was pure Ella—each positioned to catch the best light, to create privacy without isolation. The beautifully restored dark wood surfaces were bare except for place settings. No tablecloths needed when the tables themselves were art.

Eight in the morning meant the breakfast crowd was in full swing. A family with twin toddlers occupied the big round table, the parents looking both harried and grateful for the sturdy chairs and patient service. Two couples who might have been traveling together clustered near the windows, talking about testing themselves on the dune climb. A single woman read a paperback in the corner, so still she might have been furniture.

And at a table for two near the sideboard, "that" couple.

Katie didn't know their names yet, but she knew the type. Him: silver-haired and phone-focused, his free hand gesturing at air while he talked to someone who wasn't there. His coffee cooling, untouched. His wife: tidy and fading, despite the red rose blouse, trying to disappear into her chair, cutting her eggs Benedict into smaller and smaller pieces like she could divide herself into small enough portions to not take up space.

The woman wore jewelry that caught the light—silver and beach glass, Katie noticed with professional interest. Handmade, not mass-produced. The kind of pieces that took patience and love.

"I swear," Agnes muttered, appearing at Katie's elbow with a coffee pot, "Those Jenkinses. If he doesn't put that phone down soon, I'm going to accidentally trip and send his coffee right into his lap." She caught herself, smiled apologetically. "Sorry. He's been on that thing since six-thirty. She's been alone at a table for two the whole time."

Katie watched Mrs. Jenkins rearrange her eggs again, not eating, just... waiting. For what? For him to see her? For breakfast to end? For something to change?

"Beautiful jewelry she's wearing," Katie said.

Agnes's face softened. "She makes it herself. Showed me some pieces yesterday. Artists all over the place these days."

The smell of breakfast—maple syrup and fresh bread and, oh, real butter—made Katie's stomach growl.

"I hear you," Agnes said with a chuckle. "You're over here." At the bay window table, where Finn Davidson had already made his stand. Or casual lounge.

Morning light turned his dark hair almost blue-black, like crow feathers in sunshine. He hadn't seen her yet, was reading something on his phone. His charcoal henley looked soft enough to sleep in, the sleeves pushed up to reveal those forearms and that tree tattoos. One looked like a ceramic glaze formula written in elegant script. Another might have been a coastline, abstract and flowing.

He looked up.

Their eyes met.

He stood—actually stood, like men did in old movies or her classic romance novels—and Katie felt heat creep up her neck. The way he moved through space, confident but not aggressive, made her more aware of her own body. Her jeans with the inevitable burn mark on the thigh. Her hands, rough from work. Her hair already escaping the bun she'd tried to make neat.

"Katie." Her name in his mouth sounded like he'd been practicing it. "Thanks for coming."

"Thanks for asking." She slid into the chair he pulled out—when was the last time someone had pulled out a chair for her?—and tried not to notice how good he smelled. Not cologne exactly, but something clean and warm, like sun-dried linen with a hint of clay dust. Earth and air, solid and ephemeral at once.

The breakfast crowd's chatter created a comfortable bubble of white noise around them. Silverware clinked against plates. Chairs scraped. Voices rose and fell. Mr. Jenkins's went on about quarterly projections.

"The fog this morning," Finn said, gesturing toward

the window where the world had turned to pearl and silver. "It's like being inside a Japanese watercolor. The way it softens every edge, makes the familiar mysterious."

Exactly. "I've always loved fog mornings here," Katie said. "The way sound travels differently. You can hear super clear, but you can't see ten feet in front of you."

"Isolation and connection at once." Finn's eyes—definitely gray with green flecks, like beach glass worn smooth—held hers. "That's what your work captures so perfectly. That duality."

Before Katie could respond, Agnes appeared with coffee and menus, her white hair pinned in its usual precise bun, her server's smile genuine for regulars like Katie.

"The usual?" Agnes asked Katie, pouring gorgeously rich smelling coffee into her cup.

Katie started to nod—black coffee and wheat toast had been her breakfast for years—but something about the way Finn studied the menu with genuine interest, the way he treated breakfast as an event rather than fuel, made her want more.

"French toast," Finn said. "And do you have orange juice? Freshly squeezed?"

"Of course." Agnes's smile widened. She knew a good tipper when she saw one. "I'll bring both."

The orange juice when it arrived smelled like Florida

sunshine. The coffee steamed with promise. Katie ordered eggs Benedict—same as Mrs. Jenkins, she noticed with a pang—instead of her usual toast. Drawn into Finn's obvious pleasure in good food, in making breakfast an occasion.

"I looked up more of your work last night," Finn said. His fingers traced the edge of his napkin as he spoke, long and elegant, artist's hands that knew how to coax beauty from raw materials. "The series you did on industrial decay and renewal. The way you made those rusted farm implements look like they were dancing."

"You found those?" Katie's chest warmed. She'd posted that series on an obscure art blog two years ago, after rejection number ten. "That was just experimentation. Playing around."

"No." Finn leaned forward, his voice dropping to something more intimate. The breakfast crowd faded. Even Mr. Jenkins's droning dimmed. "That was an artist finding her voice. The way you use patina and rust as intentional design elements rather than flaws to be hidden—it's brilliant."

Brilliant.

The word hung between them like a struck bell. Katie felt her cheeks heat. Gallery rejections had used words like "competent" and "technically proficient." Never brilliant.

At the next table, Mrs. Jenkins had stopped

pretending to eat. She stared out the window at the fog, one hand absently touching the beach glass pendant at her throat. Her husband continued his call, oblivious to the glances of irritation from other tables.

Their food arrived, Agnes arranging plates with practiced efficiency. The eggs were perfect, hollandaise like silk, the English muffin crisped just right. Katie ate slowly, savoring, drawn into Finn's obvious appreciation for the meal. He ate like he probably made art—with attention, with respect for the materials.

"Tell me about your ceramics," Katie said, needing to shift focus from the way his praise made her feel. "The wave forms especially. How do you get that translucency?"

Finn's face transformed when he talked about his craft. His hands moved as he explained his glazing technique, demonstrating the layering process in the air between them. Katie caught herself staring at those hands, imagining them shaping clay, patient and sure. The way her hands knew metal's moods, his knew earth's.

"But what I really want to explore," he said, setting down his fork, "is the intersection between our mediums. Ceramic and metal. Earth and fire. The conversations our materials could have."

"Conversations?" Katie took a sip of orange juice,

the brightness startling on her tongue. Like drinking sunshine.

"Your lighthouse sculpture—the one in your portfolio. The one outside, by the library. The way the metal captures and reflects light. Imagine that paired with ceramic pieces that absorb light, that glow from within." His eyes held hers, intense with possibility. "We could create installations that transform throughout the day as the light changes."

Katie's breath caught. He'd articulated something she'd been reaching toward but hadn't quite grasped. "Like the lighthouse itself. Pieces that look functional— basic— but become transcendent in certain conditions."

"Exactly." Finn smiled, and Katie noticed a tiny scar at the corner of his mouth, an imperfection that somehow made him more attractive. More real. "You understand. So many artists work in isolation, protecting their vision. But the best art comes from dialogue, from pushing each other toward something neither could achieve alone."

Behind him, Mr. Jenkins had finally ended his call. He looked at his wife with surprise, as if just remembering she existed. "Ruth, we should go. I have another call at nine."

Ruth Jenkins gathered her things. As she passed their table, her eyes met Katie's briefly. Recognizing another artist.

"The thing is," Finn continued, "your work deserves a bigger stage. Not," he added quickly, "that Green Arbor isn't wonderful. But Katie, you should be showing in Chicago. New York. Your techniques, your vision—they belong in conversation with the larger art world."

Katie's fork paused halfway to her mouth. "Fifteen galleries disagree with you."

"Fifteen galleries are run by people who don't understand innovation when they see it." Finn's voice carried absolute conviction. "I know gallery owners who would kill for work like yours. People who understand that the future of sculpture isn't just about scale or shock value, but about intimacy, transformation, story."

He reached across the table, not quite touching her hand but close enough that she could feel the warmth from his skin. The dark wood of the table between them suddenly seemed like an ocean.

"After this competition, regardless of who gets the position, I want to introduce you to some people. Get your work in front of eyes that will see what I see."

Katie's heart hammered against her ribs. This was what she'd dreamed of—someone with connections, someone who understood her work, someone who could open doors that had been slammed in her face. Someone who saw her as more than Liam's little sister who made nice things for tourists.

"That's... incredibly generous," she managed.

"It's not generous. It's necessary." Finn pulled his hand back, but his gaze held hers. "Art like yours shouldn't be hidden in a small town garage."

Something about the phrasing—hidden in a small town garage—sent an unexpected prickle down Katie's spine. But then Finn was smiling again, asking about her welding technique, and the moment passed.

They talked through second cups of coffee, through Agnes clearing their plates and leaving the check that Finn insisted on taking. The dining room filled and emptied around them. Katie laughed at his story about a ceramic piece that had exploded in the kiln ("looked like abstract expressionism, sold for twice what the original would have"), found herself leaning into his attention like a plant toward sun.

The family with toddlers departed in a chaos of sippy cups and fallen napkins. The tourist couples headed out to photograph the lighthouse in fog. Even the woman with her paperback finally left, marking her page carefully. But Katie barely noticed, her focus narrowed to the man across from her who spoke her language, who understood the conversation between artist and material.

"We should do this again," Finn said as they stood to leave. The fog was starting to lift outside the windows. "Maybe dinner? I know these next few days are packed with evaluation activities, but after Thursday's presentation, things ease up."

Katie's mind went blank. Dinner. With Finn. Like a date.

"There's this place," she said, her voice coming out slightly breathless. "Mama Lynx Creamery. They do amazing—"

"Actually," Finn interrupted gently, "I made inquiries about Ink. Out on the beach? Mrs. Frankl says it's extraordinary."

Ink. Katie had been there exactly once, for her parents' anniversary. White tablecloths that actually were tablecloths, not bare wood. Five courses. Wine pairings. Prices that made her wonder if they'd accidentally added an extra zero.

"My treat, of course," Finn added, perhaps reading her hesitation. "Consider it a celebration of surviving the first week of evaluation. Thursday night? Nine o'clock?"

The way he stood there, backlit by morning light through the bay window, confident and accomplished and interested in her—not just her work, but her— made Katie's careful defenses crumble.

"Yes," she heard herself say. "Thursday at nine."

Finn's smile transformed his face from handsome to devastating. "Perfect. I'll make the reservation."

He walked her to the door, his hand briefly touching

the small of her back as they navigated around a new couple checking in. The touch was light, appropriate, but Katie felt it like a brand through her shirt.

"Until then," he said at the door. "Knock 'em dead today."

"Right." Katie nodded, trying to organize her scattered thoughts. "You too."

She drove home in a daze. The taste of hollandaise lingered. Her phone, forgotten in her cup holder, showed a new text.

Ella: *DETAILS. NOW.*

Katie pulled into her driveway, staring at the message. How could she possibly explain the way Finn had looked at her work, at her? The way he'd made her feel: an artist worthy of attention, a woman who could captivate a man.

The way her skin still felt warm where he'd almost touched her hand. The dinner at Ink, the gallery connections. The way he'd called her brilliant.

Back in her workshop, she texted back: *Delicious, as usual. Finn knows a lot about contemporary metal work.*

Ella: *Did he find out about you beforehand?*

How could he?

Katie tossed her phone on the workbench and walked over to her work-in-progress. Square, red, but absolutely not a lighthouse, if she had anything to say about it.

She had three days until that dinner. Three days to prove she deserved the lighthouse position. Three days to figure out why Finn's attention made her feel like she could conquer the art world, while everybody else's careful attention made her feel... confined.

The metal waited, patient and uncomplicated.

Unlike everything else in her life.

Chapter Ten

Graham Cheever had participated in countless committee meetings in the Starlight Arbor Inn's conference room over the past five years. But this Wednesday morning's meeting felt different, as if the room itself had shifted slightly overnight.

The morning light through the windows fell at an unusual angle, creating shadows where there had previously been illumination. The air felt cooler than normal despite the June warmth outside, carrying the faint scent of rain though the skies were clear. Even the inn's usual creaks and sighs had taken on a different rhythm, like a familiar song played in a minor key.

"Three days into the evaluation period," Mrs. Frankl said, adjusting her reading glasses as she reviewed her notes, "and I must say I'm impressed with both candidates' approaches."

Graham nodded noncommittally, pen poised above his notepad. Around the table, the other committee members arranged their materials with varying degrees of organization—Mrs. Frankl's color-coded files, Jim Hartwell's leather portfolio with the State of Michigan logo, Captain Bernie's scattered notes on what appeared to be the back of grocery receipts. The coffee in Graham's cup was too strong, bitter on his tongue, but he sipped it anyway, using the sharp taste to focus his thoughts.

"Finn's community engagement session yesterday was particularly well-received," Dottie Kowalski said, her teacher's precision evident in her carefully bulleted list. "His idea for a rotating exhibition program featuring local artists alongside established names could really put Green Arbor on the cultural map."

"Katie's historical knowledge is unmatched," Captain Bernie countered, smoothing out his notes with uncharacteristic care. "Knew details about the original construction I'd forgotten myself. And the kids at yesterday's youth workshop were absolutely captivated by her metalworking demonstration."

Graham wrote each observation in his neat script, the weight of the pen familiar in his hand, the act of recording helping him maintain professional distance.

But beneath his careful notation, other observations accumulated. The way Katie's name caused a subtle shift in the room's temperature, the way Finn's proposals always seemed to incorporate her ideas while positioning his vision as the framework.

"What's most interesting," Mrs. Frankl continued, "is the natural artistic synergy developing between them. Their approaches complement each other remarkably well."

The windows rattled slightly, a breeze that shouldn't have been possible in the closed room stirring the papers on the table. No one else seemed to notice.

"Individual vision should remain our primary consideration," Graham heard himself say. So pedantic. "The position is for one lighthouse keeper."

Mrs. Frankl's gaze was too perceptive for comfort. "Of course, Graham. Though innovative partnerships should not be discounted."

The meeting continued, each committee member reviewing observations from the first three days of evaluation. Graham recorded everything, his handwriting growing smaller and more precise as the discussion progressed. Outside, clouds began to gather over the lake, the morning light dimming by imperceptible degrees.

Finally, they were out of comments, and coffee, and

Beatrice's sugar cookies. They started to gather their materials

"Tomorrow evening's community presentations will be illuminating," Mrs. Frankl said. "It's one thing to impress a committee, quite another to win over Green Arbor as a whole."

Graham nodded, tucking his notes into his well-worn satchel. Thoughts swirled like the approaching storm clouds—observations filed and cross-referenced, patterns emerging that he wasn't certain the others had noticed.

Katie's text from Monday night—*Day one down. This is really happening!*—had been followed by increasingly infrequent messages as the evaluation activities consumed her time. Graham had maintained a careful distance, limiting his responses to measured encouragement appropriate for a committee member.

But he'd watched. He's studied the subtle dynamics developing between the candidates. The way Finn consistently positioned himself as the senior partner in potential collaborations. The way Katie's initial openness was gradually giving way to a wariness she tried to hide. The way the committee seemed charmed by Finn's sophisticated vision while appreciating Katie's authentic connection to Green Arbor.

"Graham? Your thoughts?" Mrs. Frankl's voice pulled him back to the present.

"I believe both candidates are demonstrating strong qualifications," he answered, the words carefully chosen. "Tomorrow's presentations will provide valuable community perspective."

Mrs. Frankl studied him for a moment longer than necessary, something knowing in her expression. "Indeed they will."

The town hall stood at the center of Green Arbor, its white clapboard exterior and modest steeple embodying the town's blend of practicality and quiet dignity. Inside, the main meeting room echoed with Graham's footsteps as he arranged chairs in precise rows, the hollow sound emphasizing the emptiness that would soon be filled with community members.

Afternoon light streamed through tall windows, dust motes dancing in the golden beams that fell across wooden floors worn smooth by generations of town gatherings. The air smelled of lemon polish and old wood, with undertones of the coffee that would soon be brewing in the small kitchen at the back.

Graham checked his watch—5:17 PM. The presentations wouldn't begin until seven, but preparation was key to smooth execution. He methodically arranged evaluation materials on the committee table, aligning pencils and feedback forms with geometric precision.

The sound of voices drifted from the entrance hall—Katie and Finn arriving to set up their displays. Graham straightened, adjusting his tie in a habitual gesture before moving to greet them.

"Graham," Finn said with an easy smile, extending his hand. His grip was firm, confident, his casual attire somehow looking more appropriate than Graham's pressed shirt and tie. "Just the man we wanted to see. Is there a preference for how the displays should be arranged?"

"The east wall has better lighting, especially on summer evenings." Graham answered, professional courtesy overriding the tension that had become his constant companion in Finn's presence. "It's traditionally used for visual presentations."

Katie entered behind Finn, carrying a portfolio that looked heavier than the one she'd had on Monday. Her hair was pulled back more neatly than usual, her clothing a clear attempt at professionalism—dark jeans without metal stains, a green blouse that brought out her eyes. Graham cataloged these details automatically, along with the slight shadows beneath her eyes and the tension in her shoulders.

"Graham," she said, his name carrying a warmth

that hadn't been in Finn's formal greeting. "Thanks for setting everything up. The place looks good."

"Standard arrangement," he replied, though something in him warmed at her appreciation of his efforts. "The committee will sit at the front table. Presentations will be twenty minutes each, followed by community questions."

"Our collaborative vision could transform this lighthouse into a destination," Finn said, moving toward the east wall to assess the space. "We'll need room to display both conceptual drawings and material samples."

Katie's didn't seem to notice the word "our." Just turned that warm smile to Finn.

"Plenty of space to share."

"I'll leave you to your preparations," Graham said, gathering his clipboard. "The room is available until six, then will reopen at six-thirty for the event."

As he moved toward the door, he heard Finn's voice drop to a more intimate tone: "Katie, I've been meaning to ask—that welding technique you developed for textured surfaces. Would you consider demonstrating it during a workshop series? It would be the perfect complement to the ceramic relief approach I've been developing."

Graham didn't stay to hear her answer, but he noted the pattern—another request that positioned her work as complementary to Finn's vision rather than standing on its own. Another subtle nudge toward collaboration on Finn's terms.

Outside, the too-warm afternoon had grown heavy with approaching weather, humidity pressing against skin and lungs. Graham loosened his tie slightly, a small rebellion against his usual precision, and decided to seek refuge in the Roastery before returning to the bookstore. Afternoon coffee and quiet and maybe a break from competition.

The café was mostly empty at this odd hour between lunch and dinner, but the baked goods display smelled just as great. He ordered his usual—medium roast, one sugar, no room for cream—and selected a small table near the window, where he could watch Green Arbor's afternoon rhythm while gathering his thoughts.

"Mind if I join you?"

Graham looked up to find one of the inn's guests beside his table. Ruth Jenkins. She held a cup of tea in one hand and a small velvet case in the other. He'd seen her several times during the week, usually alone, occasionally with her husband trailing behind, always on his phone.

"Please," Graham gestured to the empty chair, noting the weariness around her eyes despite her careful makeup. "How are you enjoying your stay in Green Arbor?"

"The inn is lovely," Ruth said, settling across from

him. "So full of character. And the town... well, it reminds me of places that still value craftsmanship. That's becoming rare."

Graham nodded, understanding exactly what she meant. In a world of mass production and digital experiences, Green Arbor maintained its appreciation for things made by hand, with care and time.

"I've been working while we're here," Ruth continued, setting the velvet case on the table between them. "Carl's been busy with calls, and I find I need... something of my own, I suppose."

She opened the case to reveal several pieces of jewelry—delicate silver work set with beach glass in varying shades of blue and green. The pieces caught the café's warm light, the glass seeming to glow from within, the silver work intricate and precise.

"These are remarkable," Graham said, genuine appreciation in his voice. He lifted a pendant, noting the careful wire wrapping that held a piece of sea glass the exact color of Katie's eyes. "True craftsmanship."

Ruth's face transformed at the praise, years falling away as she smiled. "Thank you. I've been collecting beach glass for decades, but only started making jewelry when Carl retired. I thought it might be something we could share, hunting for pieces together on beach walks."

Her voice dripped with wistfulness. Graham glanced

toward the café's other corner, where Carl Jenkins sat alone, laptop open, talking to the air—or, more likely, a customer. Missing his wife while she sat almost within reach.

"He's always so busy," Ruth said, following Graham's gaze. "Forty years of marriage, and I still haven't learned that 'one quick call' means hours." Her laugh held more resignation than humor. "I used to paint, you know. Before we were married. Carl wrote poetry then—terrible poetry, but it was for me. Now I make a model corporate wife, and he makes calls that are never quite finished."

Maybe Carl wasn't a jewelry guy? "He's missing out," Graham said.

"When someone sees only what you do, not who you are," Ruth said quietly, gathering her jewelry with careful hands, "that's not love. That's casting. Like you're playing a role in their production instead of co-creating a life."

The words seemed to drop into Graham's chest with a thunk. Watching Katie's growing warmness around Finn, the subtle reworking of her sentences to complement his. The way her text messages had grown shorter and less frequent as the week progressed.

Before Graham could respond, the café door opened, admitting a rush of humid air and afternoon light. Carl Jenkins looked up from his laptop, checking the time with a frown.

"Ruth, there you are. It's nearly six-. I need to get back to the inn for my conference call."

Ruth gathered her case with practiced efficiency, all trace of the passionate artist disappearing behind the role of accommodating wife. "Of course, dear. I was just showing Graham my little hobby."

Carl didn't even look at the jewelry, his gaze trained on the door. "We need to go. The Richardson deal won't close itself."

As they left, Ruth turned back briefly, her eyes meeting Graham's, a small smile. "Thanks," she said.

Chapter Eleven

K atie stood in front of her display table, watching Green Arbor file into the town hall like a jury returning with a verdict.

Mrs. Kowalski from the post office, who'd bought Katie's first wind chime ten years ago and still told everyone about it. Now she studied the portfolio boards with the same sharp attention she brought to weighing packages, calculating worth.

The Hartwell family claiming the entire third row— all five kids who'd loved Monday's workshop, their parents who'd seemed so impressed then, now wearing their evaluating faces. Little Emma waved. Katie's attempt to wave back looked more like she was drowning.

Stan Murphy, who'd taught Katie to use a level

when she was eight, examining the metal samples Katie had arranged on the table. Stan's weathered fingers hovered over the patinated copper, not touching, just... assessing. Like Katie was one of her construction projects that might not be up to code.

"Quite a turnout."

Finn materialized beside her, smelling like expensive soap and confidence. His display—sleek boards with perfectly lit photographs, that iPad connected to the pull-down screen Graham had set up earlier—made her handwritten labels look like a child's school project.

"Half the town," Katie managed, throat dry as sawdust.

More than half. The Frankls from the Chinese restaurant where she'd had her tenth birthday party. Mrs. Patterson who'd hired her to fix her garden gate last summer and now sat with her arms crossed, waiting to be convinced. Tom Rodriguez from the bank who'd processed her small business loan and knew exactly how much she didn't make.

They all knew her. Had known her since she was gap-toothed and dream-drunk, talking about being a famous artist someday.

Now they'd decide if she was worth the lighthouse or just Liam's little sister playing with fire.

"You're catastrophizing," Finn said quietly, his hand brief on her elbow. Professional. Supportive. "Monday's workshop was a triumph. At the ice cream shop, I over-heard a teenager talking about it with a friend—and teenagers hate everything, right? And Tuesday's tour. Mrs. Frankl said you had them eating out of your hand with those stories about the original keeper."

Monday had been different. Kids didn't judge. They just wanted to watch metal melt.

Tuesday had been different. History was safe, facts anyone could memorize.

This was her vision. Her future. Her last chance to be something more than local color.

The coffee station. Graham, arranging sugar packets with the focus of a bomb technician. Their eyes met across the filling room. He nodded once—small, certain—then returned to his packets.

Somehow that tiny gesture steadied her more than Finn's words.

Agnes, Beatrice, and Cordelia swept in like a force of nature, claiming an entire row with the authority of women who'd been running town events since before Katie was born. Cordelia caught her eye, winked.

Katie's parents. Third row, off-center, her mother already beaming that proud look that would exist regardless of what Katie actually said. Her father scan-ning the crowd like the mayor he was, looking for allies. Good thing he'd recused himself from the final decision; he would have rigged it for sure.

More faces. More history. More weight.

Jim from the hardware store who'd sold her first welding torch.

Mrs. Mandaman who'd written her recommendation letter to Interlochen Arts Academy. Katie was still amazed that she got in; still amazed that there was such a fantastic fine-arts high school in the deep woods of northern Michigan.

There were the Davidsons, who'd commissioned that garden sculpture last year and told everyone it was "interesting."

Each face a judgment waiting to happen. Each person someone she'd have to see at the grocery store, the post office, the Roastery for the rest of her life if she failed tonight.

"Breathe," Finn murmured.

She was breathing. Sort of. In that way where oxygen went in but didn't seem to actually reach anything useful.

Mrs. Frankl approached the podium. The lavender suit, this time with a darker lavender blouse, perfectly pressed despite humidity that made Katie's hair escape her attempted bun in springs of chaos. That particular expression that meant business.

"Good evening, everyone. Thank you for joining us for this important community event."

The words blurred. Katie checked her portfolio

arrangement yet again. The lighthouse photographs—were they straight? The metal samples—did they show the progression clearly? The budget projections—had she made a calculation error that Tom Rodriguez would spot immediately?

"Our first presenter is Katie Carter."

The air left the room.

Or maybe just her lungs.

Every face turned toward her. Waiting. A hundred small-town judges who'd known her since before she could hold a welding torch. Who'd decide if she was worth their lighthouse or just playing pretend.

Katie's legs moved without permission, carrying her to the front. Her first display board—the lighthouse through seasons—trembled in her hands. The metal easel scraped against the floor like a scream.

"The lighthouse."

Her voice came out wrong. Cracked. Like she was thirteen again, presenting her first metalwork project in shop class.

Clear throat. Try again.

"The lighthouse isn't just a building."

Stan Murphy shifted in her chair. Evaluating.

"It's a promise."

The words came from somewhere deeper than her prepared speech. From the girl who'd drawn lighthouses on every surface. From the woman who'd been rejected by fifteen galleries but still was impelled to get up every morning to make metal sing.

"Every night for over a century, it promised ships they weren't alone in the dark. Promised families their loved ones had a guide home. Promised Green Arbor that some things endure."

Captain Bernie nodded slightly. Good. One down, ninety-nine to go.

Katie moved through her presentation like swimming through honey. Each board a confession. Each sample an admission of ambition. Her hands shook as she explained the workshop program, but her voice grew stronger talking about kids learning that metal wasn't just industrial—it was possibility.

Twenty minutes of exposure. Twenty minutes of standing there while everyone who'd ever known her decided if she was enough.

When the applause came, warm and genuine, Katie's knees almost buckled. Mrs. Kowalski whistled. Her father beamed. Her mother had definitely taken forty pictures.

She made it back to her chair in the front row on liquid legs as Finn took the floor.

Watching him was like watching water flow downhill. Natural. Easy. Inevitable.

No trembling hands. No cracked voice. Just smooth confidence as images flowed on the screen, his vision unfolding like he was offering them a gift they'd be foolish to refuse.

"Katie's right," he began, that smile engaging the room like they were all in on something special. "The lighthouse is a promise. But it's also an invitation."

His presentation was everything hers wasn't. Polished. Professional. Free from the weight of history and expectation because he could leave tomorrow and never see these people again.

When he talked about Katie's work—her "brilliant metal sculptures" that would dialogue with his ceramics —she felt herself shrinking. Becoming supporting cast in his production.

"Together, we could make Green Arbor's lighthouse a destination..."

Together.

We.

Like her vision was incomplete without his enhancement.

Surely he didn't mean that. She was overreacting.

The applause for Finn was louder. Mrs. Mandaman stood. Others followed.

Katie clapped too, her hands numb, watching Green Arbor choose between the girl they'd always known and the sophisticated stranger who made it all look so easy.

Then they both had to share the stage. Katie didn't feel exactly steady on her feet. Finn moved closer, so no one could see the warm hand he slid down her spine, to rest on the small of her back.

Questions followed. Stan Murphy, sharp as always: "This collaboration you keep mentioning. Is that official?"

Katie's chest tightened at Finn's smooth response about partnership opportunities, about his gallery connections opening doors for her work.

For her work.

Not her vision.

Her work, like a product he could market.

At the far end of the first row, Graham's pen moved across his notepad with mechanical precision, but his jaw had that tension she'd started recognizing. Did he think Finn's presentation had overpowered hers?

Well, it had.

What could he do about it? What could she?

Finally it ended. People surrounded them both, offering compliments that Katie accepted with a smile that felt painted on.

"You did great, sweetheart." Her father's hug smelled like sawdust and unconditional love.

"Both presentations were excellent," her mother added, though her eyes stayed on Katie. Mom had seen the shaking hands, the cracked voice, the hometown girl trying to prove she was more. "I'm so proud of you," she said.

Ugh.

Someone called out to Finn, and he turned away. The small of her back went cold.

Then Graham was there, coffee appearing in her hands—perfect temperature, perfect sweetness—and his quiet words: "Your vision for the lighthouse is exactly what Green Arbor needs."

"But is it what they want?" The question escaped before she could stop it.

His eyes found hers, steady as bedrock. "You are not a complement to someone else's vision, Katie. Your work stands alone."

The words landed in her chest like stones in still water, ripples spreading outward.

"Want some ice cream?"

She did. She so did.

Then Finn's hand on her shoulder, warm and reassuring.

"Graham," he said, that easy smile including everyone. "Great organization, as ever. If you ever want a job as a gallery manager, I know two places that would snap you up in a heartbeat."

Katie felt a flutter of pride. Finn moved in circles where people got snapped up by galleries. Where talent was recognized and rewarded. And he'd chosen to compete beside her tonight, to include her work in his vision.

Graham's expression stayed carefully neutral, but something flickered in his eyes.

"I know where I belong," he said quietly.

Something in his tone made Katie's stomach dip, though she couldn't say why. Finn squeezed her shoulder, gentle and encouraging.

"Of course. Green Arbor's lucky to have you." He turned to Katie, his gray-green eyes warm. "Ready for Ink? Reservation's at nine. We should celebrate properly after that triumph."

Triumph. He'd called her presentation a triumph.

"I—yes. Wonderful."

"The raw bar there is exceptional," Finn said, guiding her toward the door with that light touch on her back. "They fly in oysters from Prince Edward Island. You'll love them."

Katie had never had oysters from Prince Edward Island. Never had oysters flown in from anywhere. The idea that Finn wanted to share that with her, to introduce her to things she'd never experienced, made her chest warm.

"Katie?" Graham's voice, controlled but with an edge she didn't recognize.

She turned back. He stood by the coffee station, still holding the pot he'd used to pour her perfect cup earlier. His jaw had that tension again.

"Good luck tomorrow," he said. The words were

pleasant enough, but something underneath them wasn't.

"Thanks." She wanted to say more—thank him for the coffee, for his steady presence, for saying her work stood alone—but Finn was already moving toward the door, and she found herself following.

"They won't hold the reservation long," Finn said, his hand finding that spot on her back again. "Summer traffic from Chicago."

Chicago people coming to Green Arbor for dinner. People from Finn's world, the one he was opening to her.

The June night wrapped around them, thick with humidity and promise. Behind them, she heard the coffee pot set down on the table. Firmly. But Katie was already looking ahead, toward Ink's sophisticated ambiance, toward oysters from places she'd never been, toward a future that suddenly seemed bigger than Green Arbor's borders.

Finn thought she was brilliant.

Tonight, that was enough.

More than enough.

Chapter Twelve

The walk from the town hall to Ink couldn't have been more than ten minutes, but for Katie time stretched like heated metal. Down Main Street, past the darkened windows of shops she'd known her whole life. Graham's bookstore, locked and lampless. Her family's hardware store, dim while the floor above glowed; Mom and Dad already back at home. Mom had invited Katie home for lasagna—her favorite—but was delighted to hear that she already had plans.

"He seems really nice," she'd whispered to Katie while Finn was chatting with Dad abut carving tools.

Despite the cooling night breeze off Lake Michigan, Katie's feet were hot, the sidewalks retaining heat from the day. Shouldn't have worn boots tonight. The heels clicked against pavement in rhythm with Finn's confident stride, the sound surprisingly loud even with the background of crickets, slow car traffic, and people enjoying ice cream outside the creamery.

"You were magnificent," Finn said, his hand at the small of her back, guiding her around a crack in the sidewalk she could have navigated blindfolded. "The way you talked about the lighthouse as a promise—that's poetry."

Poetry. Her father built things. Her brother built things. She built things. None of them had ever been called poetry before.

Then the turn toward the beach, and past a short block of cottages, to the spot where Glen Arbor transformed.

Ink rose from the beach road like a piece of driftwood that had decided to become architecture—all weathered cedar and steel, angles that caught the dying light and threw it back sharper. The building pressed against the sand's edge as if it had grown there, its foundation practically kissing the high-tide line where Lake Michigan left its daily love notes in shells and smoothed glass.

To the north, Glen Arbor's white-sand beach stretched in a pristine arc, the kind of sand that squeaked under bare feet and made tourists forget about their real lives. Dune grass framed the restaurant's deck, planted in geometric beds that tried to look natural but were too perfect, too organized, like someone had explained wildness to an architect who'd never actually seen it. The windows—floor to ceiling, naturally—reflected the last lines of sunset in sheets of copper and gold, turning the whole building into a lighthouse of a different sort, one that guided people with disposable income toward small plates and extensive wine lists.

"I discovered this place Tuesday," Finn said, opening the door for her. "After your historical tour. Which was brilliant, by the way. The ghost stories especially."

Tuesday. While she'd been eating leftover pizza in her workshop, sketching lighthouse interpretive displays until her eyes burned, he'd been here. Discovering.

Inside, Ink assaulted her senses with its carefully orchestrated casualness—concrete floors polished to the kind of shine that made Katie wonder if people ever slipped in their fancy shoes, walls of reclaimed wood that had probably cost more than actual new wood, Edison bulbs strung at precise intervals to create ambiance that whispered rather than shouted.

The open kitchen ran along the back wall like a stage, all gleaming steel and blue flame, chefs in black moving with the kind of precision that made cooking look like surgery, each plate emerging like a small miracle of geometry and color. The bar stretched along the north wall—a single slab of some wood with a Latin name she'd never remember, bottles arranged by height and color like a booze rainbow, backlit to make even vodka look mysterious.

The scents were layered with intention: wood smoke from the pizza oven that probably had a fancier name, truffle oil that haunted the air like an expensive ghost, the sharp tang of microgreens, and underneath it all, the lake—because even Ink's filtered air system couldn't completely erase Michigan.

The sound design was just as intentional—conversation pitched at confession level, jazz that apologized for existing, the periodic satisfying pop of a cork being pulled, the subtle symphony of silverware against plates that cost more than her monthly grocery budget. Every table was positioned to see the lake without seeing other tables directly, privacy and views in perfect, pricey balance.

"Mr. Davidson," the hostess purred. Actually purred. "Your usual table?"

His usual table. Three days in Glen Arbor and he had a usual table.

Katie followed, hand over the tiny burn hole on the thigh of her black jeans. Her good blouse that had seemed professional an hour ago and now felt like playing dress-up. The other diners looked assembled rather than dressed—carefully curated casual that probably cost more than her monthly welding supply budget.

Their table—Finn's usual table—commanded the best view. Lake Michigan stretched beyond the windows, going purple with dusk. The lighthouse was only a suggestion, a shadow, a darker purple against the sky. She wished the bright beam was on, but since the decommissioning the lighthouse was more dark than light.

"The wine list," Finn said to the server who materialized beside them. Male, young, cheekbones that could cut glass. "And tell Sven we'll do the tasting menu."

The tasting menu.

Katie had looked at Ink's website once, after it opened last year. The tasting menu cost more than she made on a good day at the farmers market.

"Finn, I should—"

"My treat," he said, that smile warming his storm-cloud eyes. "We're celebrating. Your triumph, and mine. Our triumph."

That word again. Triumph. It tasted unfamiliar, like the amuse-bouche that appeared without ordering—something architectural on a spoon that the server described with words Katie recognized individually but not in combination.

"Compressed watermelon," Finn translated, lifting his spoon. "With sheep's milk feta and black lime."

Katie put the whole thing in her mouth because that seemed safest. Flavors exploded—sweet, salt, sour, something else entirely. Not unpleasant, but not anything her mouth recognized as food.

"Nice, huh?" Finn said.

"Wow."

"Your first molecular gastronomy experience?" Finn's smile gentled the observation.

"My first a lot of things," she admitted.

The wine arrived. Finn discussed it with the server in a language that sounded like English but wasn't, not really. Terroir and tannins and vintage years that meant something to them but slid past Katie like water off hot metal.

"Trust me," Finn said, after the server poured something golden into her glass. "This will change how you think about wine."

She sipped. It tasted like... wine. Good wine, probably, though her experience was limited to whatever someone brought to backyard barbecues. But Finn watched her expectantly, so she smiled and made an appreciative sound.

"You taste the minerality?" he asked. "The volcanic soil comes through beautifully."

Volcanic soil. In wine. Sure.

"Tell me about your piece for that hotel in New York," Katie said, desperate to shift to territory she understood. "The installation you mentioned. The one with the wave forms."

His face transformed, animation replacing evaluation. As he talked—about reduction firing and ash glazes, about the conversation between earth and sky—Katie found herself leaning forward. This she understood. The obsession with process, the endless experimentation, the sweet spot where control met chaos and made something unprecedented.

The first course arrived. Scallops, the server announced, though they looked nothing like the scallops her mother pan-fried with butter. These perched on shells like pearls, topped with something green and something orange and something that looked like edible flowers.

"Uni," Finn identified the orange. "Sea urchin. Acquired taste, but worth acquiring."

It tasted like low tide. Like licking the barnacles off pier posts. Katie swallowed, smiled, reached for wine to wash away the ocean flooding her mouth.

"So," Finn said, dissecting his scallop with surgical precision, "tell me about the galleries. The fifteen rejections."

The wine turned to copper in her throat. "How did you—"

"Katie." His hand covered hers on the table. "You told me that. Besides, rejection is part of the process. My first fifty applications were rejected."

Fifty. The number should have been comforting. Instead, it made her fifteen feel insignificant. Amateur.

"The difference," he continued, "is knowing how to frame your work. Your technical skills are exceptional, but galleries need narrative. They need to understand where you fit in the contemporary conversation."

"I thought my work would speak for itself."

"Art never speaks for itself." He squeezed her hand before releasing it. "It needs context. Translation. That's what I can offer—introducing your work to people who understand the vocabulary."

More courses arrived. Each one a tiny architecture, described in paragraphs, consumed in bites. Finn guided her through them like a docent, explaining flavor profiles and techniques, which fork to use (why were there so many forks?), how to appreciate the negative space on the plate.

"You're laughing at me," she said, catching his smile as she struggled with something that might have been fish or might have been performance art.

"I'm charmed by you," he corrected. "You're so authentic, Katie. So unaffected. It's refreshing."

Unaffected. Was that good? It sounded like something you'd say about a child.

A couple entered the restaurant, the woman's laughter carrying like dropped crystal. Chicago people,

Katie could tell by their clothes, their confidence, the way they owned space instead of apologizing for occupying it.

"Finn?" The woman's voice carried delight and surprise. "Finn Davidson?"

They descended on the table like beautiful birds of prey. The woman, all sharp angles and statement jewelry. The man, silver-haired and suited despite the June heat.

"Margot, Richard." Finn stood, air-kissed, shook hands. "What brings you to the wilderness?"

"Weekend place in Leland," Richard said, but his eyes had found Katie. "And you? Scouting for the Krasnoff Prize?"

"Something like that." Finn's hand found Katie's shoulder. "This is Katie Carter. Extraordinary metalwork artist. Katie, Margot and Richard Pellinger. They own one of Chicago's most innovative galleries."

"Metalwork," Margot's interest sharpened. "Contemporary? Traditional?"

"Both," Finn answered before Katie could. "She's developed revolutionary techniques with patina and texture. Transforms industrial materials into pure poetry."

There was that word again. Poetry.

"Interesting." Richard studied Katie like she was one of the architectural plates. "Are you represented?"

"Not yet," Finn said. Still answering for her. "We're exploring options."

We.

"Send me images," Margot said, producing a card from thin air. "We're looking for emerging voices for our fall showcase."

They drifted away, leaving cologne and possibility in their wake. Katie held the card—thick, letterpress, important.

"That," Finn said, lifting his wine glass, "is how it happens. One conversation. One connection. Your whole trajectory changes."

The main course arrived. Lamb, pink as dawn, arranged with things Katie couldn't identify but that looked like tiny vegetables attending court. It tasted like butter and earth and something indefinably sophisticated.

"The Pellingers could change everything for you," Finn continued. "Their spring showcase launches careers. Of course, you'd need to refine your artist's statement. Develop a cohesive portfolio. Consider your market position."

Market position.

Katie thought about her workshop. Her half-finished lighthouse. The way metal sang when she got the temperature exactly right.

"I just want to make good work," she said.

"Good work isn't enough." Finn's tone was gentle, patient. "Talent isn't enough. You need strategy. Connections. Someone who understands the system."

"Someone like you."

"Exactly like me." He smiled, reached across to adjust her wine glass, turning it so the etching faced outward. "Small things matter, Katie. Presentation. Context. The story you tell about your work."

Dessert arrived without consultation. Chocolate something with gold leaf and a sauce painted on the plate like Japanese calligraphy. It tasted like excellence and looked like rent money.

"I should tell you," Finn said as Katie tried to eat gold leaf without looking like she was eating gold leaf, "the lighthouse position is secondary for me."

Katie nearly choked on gold leaf.

"Don't misunderstand—I want it. The studio space, the platform, the opportunity to create something significant here. But what I really want is to help launch deserving artists. Artists like you."

Katie swallowed, hard. "That's... generous."

"It's practical." He leaned forward, intent. "Your work deserves better than craft fairs and local commissions. You should be in museums, Katie. Private collections. International exhibitions."

The words painted pictures. Katie Carter at gallery openings. Katie Carter in art magazines. Katie Carter mattering beyond Green Arbor's borders.

"With your talent and my connections," Finn continued, "we could build something extraordinary. Whether that's here at the lighthouse or somewhere else entirely."

Somewhere else entirely.

The check arrived in a leather folder that looked like it should contain state secrets. Finn signed without looking at the total.

"Shall we walk?" he suggested. "The beach is beautiful at night."

Outside, back into the thick summer air after Ink's controlled climate. They walked toward the water, but Katie stopped at the top of the beach. She dropped down the the curb in front of the weekly newspaper's metal box, and stripped off her boots and socks. She set them them in the space by the box where everybody else had left theirs.

Finn watched her but didn't make a move to remove his fancy soft loafers.

Katie looked up at him and smiled. "Beaches are for feet."

He sighed. "I suppose." He slipped out of his shoes without sitting, and tucked his thin socks into the toes.

He carried them with him as they stepped onto the beach.

The sand between her toes was forgiveness itself—cool on top where the night had kissed it, still warm underneath where it remembered the day. Katie's feet knew this beach like her hands knew metal, finding the firm parts without thought, avoiding the soft sinkholes where beach grass had given up.

The lake exhaled against the shore in welcome, each wave a small homecoming, and for a moment she forgot everything—the gallery owners, the gold leaf, the way Finn had ordered for her. This was real: the squeak of perfect Michigan sand, the way moonlight turned foam to lace, the particular summer symphony of water meeting land meeting sky. She could taste the lake on the air, not sea-urchin ocean but something mineral and ancient and hers.

A piece of driftwood caught her eye—twisted smooth, would make a perfect base for that sculpture she'd been imagining—and she bent to examine it, running her fingers along its water-carved curves, already seeing how copper might crown it, how—

"Careful of splinters."

Finn's voice crashed over her like one of those rogue waves that came from nowhere, soaking you when you thought you were safe. His hand on her elbow, steadying her from a stumble she hadn't made. The driftwood suddenly just looked like dead wood, and she was aware again of everything—her sandy feet probably looked ridiculous, her hair was definitely a nightmare in this humidity, she'd just been crouching on a beach like a kid looking for treasure while a man who knew gallery owners waited with his Italian loafers dangling from his fingers like surrender flags.

"It's been weathered smooth," she said, straightening, but she left the driftwood where it lay.

"You were nervous tonight," Finn said. "At dinner."

"It's not my world."

"It could be." He stopped walking, turned to face her. In the moonlight, his eyes looked like mercury. He reached a hand to her face, traced the strong line of her jaw. "Magnificent."

Katie leaned into the touch. So warm, like the sand underneath.

"Katie," he said, soft. "You don't have to be the girl who makes wind chimes for tourists, You could be so much more."

The girl who makes wind chimes.

Is that how he saw her?

She pulled away from him.

"I should get home," she said. "Long day tomorrow."

"Of course."

He walked her back to her truck, parked behind

the hardware store where she'd left it that afternoon. His hand found her elbow as she climbed in, steady and possessive. "Thank you for dinner. For trusting me."

"Thank *you* for dinner," she corrected. "For the connections. For believing in my work."

"I believe in you," he said, and for a moment, in the dim light, he looked like every dream she'd had about escape, about mattering, about being chosen.

She drove home with the taste of gold leaf and possibility on her tongue.

Her workshop sat dark and patient, smelling of metal and motor oil and home. The lighthouse sculpture watched from its workbench, accusing in the moonlight streaming through windows.

Katie picked up her torch, then set it down.

Picked up Margot Pellinger's card.

Set it down.

Her phone buzzed. Graham: *Hope dinner went well. The poetry section reorganized itself again. Thought you should know.*

The poetry section. Their old joke from when she'd helped him reshelf after a particularly chaotic tourist season. The poetry never stayed where you put it, like it had opinions about alphabetical order.

She started to type back, then stopped. What would she say? That she'd eaten gold? That she'd met gallery owners? That Finn thought she could be more than the girl who makes wind chimes?

That she wasn't sure if being more meant becoming less?

Katie put the phone in her pocket without responding. The metal waited, patient and honest, ready to transform.

Chapter Thirteen

The lighthouse sculpture had grown teeth overnight.

Katie stood in her workshop at mid-morning, temple throbbing with each heartbeat, staring at the metal that had somehow rearranged itself into something sharper, angrier, more honest than she'd left it. The copper edges she'd smoothed yesterday now jutted like accusations. The base, which had been flowing and organic, had crystallized into something that looked like it could cut.

Even her art was judging her.

The inside of her mouth tasted like she'd been licking expensive ashtrays. Her stomach rolled with the ghost of sea urchin and volcanic soil. Somewhere behind her left eye, a tiny man with a very large hammer was trying to escape her skull.

White wine headache. Her first real wine headache, because whatever they'd been drinking at backyard barbecues all these years hadn't been wine, not according to Finn's standards.

Margot Pellinger's tiny business card sat heavy on her workbench. The card looked wrong here, too pristine for a surface scarred by years of toil and struggle.

Her phone buzzed. Three texts from Finn, sent at intervals through the night like he'd been composing them between courses of his own thoughts.

She didn't open them.

Not yet.

The torch sat heavy in her hand when she picked it up, the weight all wrong, like trying to write with someone else's pen. She set it down. The metal could wait. First, she needed coffee that didn't come from Liam's ancient Mr. Coffee that he'd probably inherited from his Dad, who'd probably bought during the Reagan administration.

The Roastery.

Then the hardware store.

Then figure out how to be Katie Carter again.

The bell above the Roastery door was a knife to her skull. Bad enough that it was so blasted bright outside. Beautiful high-summer day, bah.

Katie winced, pushing her sunglasses up into the mess of her hair, but the damage was done. The cheerful chime echoed between her ears like a critique of every life choice she'd made in the last twelve hours. The last twelve years.

The coffee smell that usually meant comfort and home now made her stomach consider full revolution. Too rich. Too complex. Too much like things that cost more than they should and tasted like disappointment.

"Rough night at Ink?"

Ezra stood behind the counter, his knowing smile somehow both sympathetic and amused. Of course he knew. Everyone probably knew. Green Arbor's newest sport: watching Katie Carter try to be something she wasn't.

"Coffee," she managed. "Black. Two sugars."

"The usual."

The usual. Such a simple phrase. Such a relief.

But her regular table by the window was occupied by tourists, their hiking maps spread across the scarred wood surface like they owned it. Katie found another spot, corner table, darker. Better for her headache anyway.

She was contemplating whether she could survive

the walk to the hardware store when movement caught her eye. That woman from the inn, Ruth Jenkins, alone at a table near the fireplace, bent over something small and delicate. Her hands moved with the careful precision Katie recognized—maker's hands, creating something from nothing.

Katie had started walking over before she'd consciously decided to.

"Those are beautiful."

Ruth looked up, startled, then smiled. It transformed her face, years falling away. "You're the metal artist. I saw your presentation last night."

"Katie." She gestured to the empty chair. "May I?"

"Ruth, Please." Ruth shifted her supplies—tiny pliers, rolls of silver wire, beach glass sorted by color in a sectioned container that probably had a specific name. "I saw you at Ink last night too. With that handsome ceramicist."

Katie's stomach did something complicated. "Finn. He's... we're both finalists for the lighthouse position."

"Ah." Ruth held up a piece she was working on—silver wrapped around beach glass the color of fog. "My husband used to love watching me work. Said it was like seeing thoughts become tangible."

Used to.

"He doesn't anymore?"

Ruth's laugh was soft, resigned. "Now he loves what

it represents. That his wife has an appropriate hobby. Something to discuss at dinner parties." She set down the piece, picked up another. "There's a difference, you know. Between someone collecting you and someone seeing you."

The words landed in Katie's chest like stones in still water.

Collecting you.

"This piece," Ruth continued, holding up a pendant that seemed to capture light and hold it, "I think I'm going to keep it."

"It's gorgeous." Katie's headache was easing, the tiny hammer man taking a break. Real conversation, real coffee, real understanding. "What's the stone?"

"Not a stone. Sea glass."

"I've not seen that color before."

Ruth looked up and grinned. "Found it on Ocean Beach." Then her smile fell away. "During a sales conference."

Katie was about to ask Ruth where her husband was when he walked back into the Roastery. He scowled as he passed Ezra, who didn't seem to notice. Ezra must've told him about the no loud phone calls rule.

"I should go," Katie said before he got there. She was probably in his seat. "Work shift at the hardware store."

"The hardware store." Ruth smiled. "Your father's quite proud of you, you know. He was at the town hall yesterday, talking Clint's ear off about his daughter the artist."

His daughter the artist.

Not the girl who makes wind chimes.

The walk from the Roastery to the hardware store somehow ended up at Graham's bookstore, a block beyond. Katie's feet followed the familiar path while her brain tried to process Ruth's words. The sun was aggressive, too bright, making her sunglasses necessary armor against a world that insisted on being cheerful.

The bookstore door was propped open. Graham was in the window, literally in it, arranging a new display.

"Local Artists," the sign read. Not in quotes. Not with qualifiers. Just fact.

Katie stopped, watching him work. He'd changed from long-sleeved button-downs to short sleeves, and it didn't look like he had anything on underneath. With the overhead display lights melding with the bright sun, his light blue shirt was nearly transparent. There was nothing rough about Graham, but man, was he cut. Suddenly, Katie remembered that he ran almost every day.

He was almost done. two short corner bookshelves held books about creativity, about finding your voice, about the importance of place in art. Between them, against the white of the back display wall, photographs from various Green Arbor artists through the years. Including one of her lighthouse sculptures from three years ago, before she'd learned to doubt herself.

"Changing it up," she said, stepping through the open doorway.

He turned, nearly hitting his head on the window frame. "Katie. Hi."

"Coffee run before hardware store duty." She held up her cup like evidence.

"Ah." He climbed out of the window with more grace than she would have managed, especially hungover. "Actually, I have something for you. Not ordered. Just... found."

He disappeared into the stacks, returning with a slim volume. "Women Who Work with Fire: Poems." The cover was singed at the edges, whether by design or accident she couldn't tell.

"Where did you even find this?"

"Poetry section." His mouth quirked. "It was filed under S. For Stubborn, apparently."

She laughed, and the tiny hammer man in her head set down his tools entirely.

"The poetry section reorganized itself again last

night," Graham continued, gesturing toward the back of the store. "Complete rebellion. Neruda is consorting with Bukowski. *The Lynx Path: Poems of Michigan* somehow wandered from nature poetry to nestle beside the love sonnets. Dickinson's taken over an entire shelf and appears to be holding Frost hostage."

"Probably plotting something."

"Must be." He paused, studying her face with that careful attention he brought to everything. "Rough night?"

"Rich night." The honesty surprised her. "Turns out I don't actually like the taste of gold leaf."

Graham's expression shifted, something knowing flickering in his eyes. "Sometimes the most revolutionary thing is to stay exactly who you are."

"Even if who you are is just a small-town metalworker?"

"Especially then." He moved back to his window display, adjusting a photograph so it caught the light better. "The world has plenty of people trying to be someone else. Not enough people brave enough to be themselves."

A customer entered, breaking the moment. Graham shifted into bookstore owner mode, helping them find something about native plants. Katie watched him work, noticed things she'd been not-noticing for years. The way his hands moved when he was passionate about something, gesturing with controlled enthusiasm. The way stray light caught in his glasses, making him squint slightly. The way he remembered exactly where everything was, not because he'd memorized it but because he genuinely cared about each book finding its right person.

"I should go," she said when the customer left. "Dad needs me at the store."

"You are doing great." Graham said, and then quickly corrected himself. "Both of you are."

"Good job, Lighthouse Committee."

"Sunday's presentation should be interesting."

"That's one word for it."

She was at the door when he spoke again. "Katie? The poetry book. Page thirty-seven."

The hardware store embraced her with its familiar smells—metal and oil and sawdust and the Old Spice her father had worn since before she was born. Mom stood behind the register, looking up with that expression that could diagnose emotional states from forty paces.

"You look like you need ibuprofen."

"Already took some." Katie tied on her hardware

store apron, the weight of it settling across her shoulders like armor. "Where do you need me?"

"Garden section's a disaster. Summer people"

Summer people. Folks from Chicago pretending they have the time to start a garden.

The physical work helped. Hauling bags of mulch used muscles that fancy dinners didn't require. Mixing paint gave her hands something to do besides remember how Finn had positioned them on her wine glass. The honest transaction of tools for money—this costs this much, it does this thing, thank you, have a nice day— was so simple after last night's performance.

"Katie!"

Stan Murphy stood in the fastener aisle, holding a box of screws like he was evaluating their moral character.

"Hey, Stan."

"Saw you at the town hall." Stan's weathered face gave away nothing. "Your lighthouse ideas. They make sense. Practical."

Practical. From Stan Murphy, that was a Nobel Prize.

"That other fellow." Stan selected his screws with the focus of a surgeon. "Fancy ideas. Pretty pictures. But what happens when something breaks? Can he fix it? Can he maintain it through a Michigan winter?"

Katie thought of Finn's soft hands, his perfect manicure.

"I don't know."

"You can." Stan moved toward the register. "You fixed my garden gate. Still holding strong. That's what matters. Things that last."

Things that last.

Her phone had been buzzing all afternoon. Finally, on her break, sitting on the loading dock with a sandwich from Mom that tasted like real food, Katie opened Finn's texts.

The first was thoughtful, suggesting ways to "strengthen" her presentation.

The second included photos of ceramic pieces that would "complement" her metalwork.

The third was a mock-up of a joint artist statement.

She read it twice, her sandwich turning to cardboard in her mouth.

Her work was described as "raw" and "primitive." His as "refined" and "sophisticated." Together, they would create a "dialogue between instinct and intellect."

Instinct and intellect.

Like she was all feeling and no thought.

Like she was the wild thing he could tame and display.

Was that what he had seen in her last night? When? She didn't remember acting like a feral thing.

She started to text back.

Deleted it.

Maybe he was just bad at texting. He couldn't mean it.

Started to text again.

Deleted it.

Went back inside.

A customer needed help finding the right hinge for a gate they were building. Amateur work, they admitted, almost apologetically. But their eyes shone when they described their plans, their vision for something they would create with their own hands.

Katie found them the perfect hinge. Showed them how to install it. Watched them leave with the satisfaction of someone about to make something real.

That's when it hit her.

She'd been apologizing for being "just" a small-town metalworker.

But these people—her people—they understood making things that last. They understood that creation wasn't about galleries or reviews or gold leaf. It was about transformation. About taking raw materials and making something useful, beautiful, lasting.

She texted Finn: *Breakfast tomorrow at the inn?*
He texted back immediately: *Same time, same place*
Time to let him see the real Katie Carter.

185

Chapter Fourteen

Saturday morning, Katie pulled on her good overalls, the ones without burns or metal splatter, the ones she wore to the hardware store when she wanted to look like she took the job seriously. Blue denim, soft from a hundred washes, with brass hardware that caught the light just right.

A statement.

Not trying to be anything other than Katie Carter who worked with fire and sold people the tools to fix their own lives.

She braided her hair tight, no wisps to escape and soften her face. Finn's texts glowed on her phone screen —"primitive" and "raw" and "instinct versus intellect" —each word a small blade between her ribs. She read them again, letting them cut, letting herself feel the sharp edge of being misunderstood by someone she'd almost let matter.

The poetry book lay open on her workbench, page thirty-seven dog-eared now, the words memorized but worth seeing again:

"She built herself from flame and iron,
No apologies for the sparks she threw."

No apologies.

The drive to the Inn was all windows down, June-almost-July air thick with possibilities. The Dune Festival setup had started—she passed the Kowalskis arranging their booth, Jim hauling tables from his truck, Ezra and Rosemary carrying boxes that probably contained enough baked goods to feed an army. Her people, preparing for their day.

Susan Murphy looked up from where she was hammering booth frames together, raised a hand in greeting. Katie waved back, the gesture grounding her. These people knew her. Saw her. Had watched her fail and try and fail and keep trying.

The Inn rose from its perch like something from a storybook, morning light making it glow. Pretty as a picture.

Pictures lied.

Ella stood in the doorway before Katie could knock, concern written in every line of her sister-in-law's face.

How could she know?

Innkeeper magic. Katie shook her head.

"You sure about this?" Ella said.

"Very."

The sand globe in the foyer swirled dark, agitated, like storm clouds gathering in glass. Katie watched it for a moment, wondering if the Inn was trying to encourage her or warn her.

Bacon and maple syrup competed with something else—cologne, expensive and assertive, already claiming space in the morning air.

His laugh carried from the dining room. That performance laugh, the one that invited you to be audience rather than participant.

Katie walked into the dining room. It looked exactly the same and completely different.

Same blue willow china that had witnessed generations of meals. Same botanical prints precise on cream walls. Same mahogany sideboard gleaming with care.

But Katie saw it all differently now. The china looked fragile, like it would shatter if you spoke truth near it. The morning light through tall windows felt like interrogation rather than invitation. Even the wooden floor seemed to creak warnings under her boots.

Fewer guests than Thursday. Weekend people sleeping off their Friday nights. The corner table where Ruth Jenkins had cut her eggs into smaller and smaller pieces stood empty, ghost of a marriage haunting the space.

Finn commanded the bay window table like he'd planted a flag in it.

He looked up from his phone—of course he was on his phone—and smiled. The practiced one, the one that showed exactly the right amount of teeth, the one that probably worked on gallery owners and graduate students and anyone who hadn't spent their life learning the difference between performance and truth.

He stood.

Choreography again, hitting his marks.

"Katie." He said her name like he was tasting wine, deciding if it was worth swallowing. "You look... comfortable this morning."

That pause before "comfortable." He'd wanted to say something else. Casual, maybe. Or disappointing.

She didn't wait for him to pull out her chair. Did it herself, the wood scraping against floor in a sound like accusation. Sat with space between her and the table. Room to move.

Room to leave.

Agnes appeared with coffee pot raised like a question.

"We'll have the orange juice," Finn started, "and—"

"Just the coffee for me." Katie's voice cut clean through his assumption.

Agnes's tiny nod of approval as she poured warmed Katie more than the coffee would. Finn's face did something complicated—surprise and irritation having a quick battle before his features smoothed back into concerned interest.

"Of course." He adjusted his napkin, a precise movement that bought him time to recalibrate. "You seem tense."

"I read your texts."

The words dropped between them like metal on stone.

"My texts?" His confusion was almost convincing.

"About my 'primitive' work. My 'raw' aesthetic. The 'dialogue between instinct and intellect.'"

Katie's heartbeat lived in her throat now, but her hands stayed steady on the coffee cup. The ceramic was warm, real, honest. Unlike everything else at this table.

"You misunderstood." His voice took on that patient tone, the one you used with children or difficult gallery visitors. "Primitive as in primal. Essential. Connected to something ancient and authentic. It's a compliment."

The words slid over her like oil on water. Pretty. Meaningless. Refusing to stick.

Agnes returned with menus. Finn opened his immediately.

"The eggs Benedict were exceptional on Thursday," he said. "Should we—"

"Toast." Katie didn't open her menu. "Wheat. With cherry jam."

"Just toast?" His so-manicured eyebrows did something that probably charmed people who didn't know better.

"Just toast."

The morning sun through the bay window shifted, leaving Finn in shadow while Katie sat in a pool of golden light. Agnes's pencil scratched against her order pad, the sound loud as judgment in the morning quiet. She left them with a swirl of white hair and unspoken support.

Finn's hand started across the table, reaching for hers. Katie pulled back, tucking both hands around her coffee cup. His fingers drummed once, twice, against the wood. Controlled irritation pretending to be casual rhythm.

"Katie." Her name again, but different. Careful. Like approaching a spooked animal. "I think we need to discuss tomorrow's presentation."

"I have a question first." The coffee tasted bitter and perfect. "Do you actually see my work, or just how it fits into yours?"

His face rearranged itself into concern so quickly she almost missed the flash of annoyance underneath.

"Of course I see your work. That's why I'm so excited about our collaborative possibilities. Your authenticity combined with my experience—"

"Your experience." She set down her cup, the click against saucer sharp. "My authenticity. Like I'm some natural resource you discovered."

"That's not—" He stopped, regrouped. "The art world has certain expectations. I can help you meet them. Refine your story. Present your work in a context that—"

"Whose context?"

The question hung between them while normal breakfast sounds continued around them. Forks against plates. Murmuring conversations. Chairs softly scraping. The world going on while hers shifted on its axis.

"Katie." Patient again. So patient. "You are talented. Extraordinarily talented. But talent without proper guidance, without understanding how to position yourself in the contemporary dialogue—"

"I need to be positioned?"

"We all do." He leaned forward, earnest now, selling something. "The Pellingers were very interested in our combined vision. Of course, we'd need to refine your story. Maybe downplay the small-town angle, emphasize your technical innovation instead."

Downplay.

The word sat in her stomach like cold metal.

"Downplay the place that made me."

"Not downplay. Just... reframe. You're more than just a small-town metalworker, Katie."

Just.

There it was.

Katie leaned back as the toast arrived. Plain wheat bread, butter in a small crock, cherry jam that Beatrice made every July. Katie spread butter slowly, watching it melt into warm bread, then added jam with the kind of focus she usually reserved for welding.

Finn watched her like she was performing some incomprehensible ritual.

She took a bite. It tasted like Green Arbor. Like Sunday mornings at her parents' table. Like the inn's strawberry patch and butter from the dairy two towns over and wheat from Michigan fields.

It tasted like home.

It tasted like enough.

"You want me to be less myself to be more worthy."

The words came out calm, clear, surprising them both.

"I want you to reach your potential."

"My potential or your vision of it?"

His silence stretched like heated metal, thin and telling.

Katie looked at him fully then. Really looked. Beautiful face, perfect hands that had never been burned or cut or scarred by making something real. Eyes that saw her work as material to be shaped rather than expression to be honored.

He didn't know the smell of metal cooling.

Didn't know the satisfaction of fixing something broken.

Didn't know the weight of a torch in your hand at dawn, the promise of transformation.

Didn't know her at all.

"The Pellingers—" he started.

"Are interested in something that doesn't exist." Katie stood, her toast half-eaten, her coffee mostly full. The overalls that had seemed like armor now just felt like truth. "I'll present my work tomorrow. You present yours."

"Katie, don't be naive." Something harder in his voice now, the patience finally cracking. "This is how the art world works. Connections. Collaborations. Compromises."

"Then maybe I don't want the art world."

She turned toward the door, work boots decisive on wood that had supported generations of Green Arbor meals, Green Arbor celebrations, Green Arbor truths.

"Katie!"

She didn't turn back.

The door to the dining room swung open before she reached it—not dramatically, just enough that she didn't have to pause, didn't have to push, could walk straight through like the inn itself was clearing her path. Behind her, she heard Finn's chair scrape as he stood, heard him collide with a suddenly-extended serving cart that hadn't been there seconds before.

"Oh!" Agnes exclaimed. "Where did that come from?"

The drive down the inn's steep driveway and the three blocks to the hardware store took twenty minutes. They'd already cordoned off part of Main Street for the festival, and everyone was being re-routed.

When she finally got to the hardware store, the sounds outside were booming. Hammering and laughter and someone testing the sound system with staticky bursts of music. Her people, preparing for their day of celebrating who they were, not who someone else thought they should be.

Katie went upstairs to see if Mom had any of the good coffee left.

Her phone buzzed in her pocket.

She didn't check it.

Chapter Fifteen

The hardware store booth smelled like promise and WD-40.

Katie stood behind the table of demonstrations—how to properly season cast iron, basic home repairs, the right drill bit for different materials—breathing in the familiar cocktail of metal and oil and her father's aftershave. The overalls were gone, replaced by the sundress her mother had insisted she keep in the store's break room "for emergencies."

Apparently, emotional liberation counted as an emergency.

The dress was nothing special. Soft blue cotton, tiny flowers that might have been forget-me-nots, hem that hit just above her knees. But after days of performing someone else's vision of her, the simple dress felt like revolution.

"You look happy," her mother said, not really a question.

"I am."

The festival sprawled along Main Street in organized chaos. The Kowalskis' booth of Michigan cherries gleamed like rubies. Stan Murphy was demonstrating chainsaw art with disturbing enthusiasm. Mrs. Morrison was selling her hand-carved lynx figurine. And Agnes, Beatrice, and Cordelia had claimed an entire corner for their famous hot-cross buns that would disappear before noon.

And among the crowds of summer people, her people. Not people playing at small-town charm. Not tourists hunting authenticity. Her people, who knew her name and her story and loved her anyway.

Maybe because.

"Katie!" little Emma Hartwell ran up, dragging her mother behind. "Are you doing the welding demonstration?" the little spark said.

"At three," Katie promised. "Want to be my assistant?"

Emma's squeal could have shattered glass. Pure joy, no performance required.

The crowd thickened as the sun climbed. Katie fell into a comfortable rhythm—explaining tools, sharing tips, accepting compliments about Thursday's presentation from people who'd been there, who'd seen both visions and had opinions about which one belonged.

She was demonstrating proper hammer weight for different jobs when the crowd shifted.

Not dramatically. Just that subtle adjustment that happened when something worth noticing arrived.

Graham.

But not Graham as she knew him. Not pressed khakis and careful distance Graham.

This Graham wore jeans. Actual jeans, faded and soft-looking, that sat low on his hips in a way that made Katie's mouth go dry. A grey t-shirt that had no business fitting that well, showing shoulders she'd somehow never noticed despite years of watching him shelve books. His hair wasn't perfectly controlled. His glasses caught the sun.

He carried a box that looked heavy, muscles in his forearms flexing with the weight.

Forearms. Graham had forearms.

Graham had everything.

"Where do you want the display copies?" he asked her father, but his eyes found Katie's over the crowd.

"Back table," her father said, then louder, "Look at that! Graham Cheever doing manual labor!"

"I lift books all day, Robert." Graham's voice carried

that dry humor she'd always appreciated but suddenly heard differently. "Practically an athlete."

He set the box down, and his shirt rode up.

Just a flash. Just a glimpse of skin above his waistband.

Katie forgot what she was demonstrating.

"The hammer?" Mrs. Patterson prompted, amused.

Right. Hammer. Tools. Hardware store. Not Graham's hip bone.

She fumbled through the rest of the demonstration while Graham helped her father arrange the books—guides to home repair, gardening, the kind of practical knowledge that kept life running. He'd closed the bookstore—festival folk weren't much for reading—but he tucked his wares in the other booths, just in case a reader wandered by.

He moved differently here, easier, like festival Graham was someone he only let out on special occasions.

Or maybe she was only seeing him now.

"Nice dress," he said when the crowd dispersed, voice low enough that only she heard.

"Nice jeans."

The words were out before she could stop them. Heat flooded her face, but Graham smiled. Not his careful bookstore smile. Something warmer. Dangerous.

"The poetry section behaved itself this morning," he

said, leaning against their table in a way that made the gesture look like art. "Suspicious."

"Plotting?"

"Definitely plotting." His eyes held hers. "How was breakfast?"

The question was casual. The intensity behind it wasn't.

"Educational," Katie said. "I learned I don't actually like eggs Benedict."

"Good to know what you don't like." Graham straightened, and she caught his scent—soap, old paper, and cedar, honest and real. "Helps clarify what you do."

Before she could parse that, someone called his name. The library booth needed help. He left with a small smile that felt like a promise. Katie watched him go.

Watched his shoulders.

Watched his back.

Watched—

"Katie." Her mother's voice held barely suppressed delight. "Your face is doing something interesting."

"Shut up."

"I'm just saying, Graham looks good in jeans."

"Mom!"

"What? I have eyes. Your father looked like that once. Still does, sometimes, when he—"

"I'm going to demonstrate welding now," Katie

announced to no one. "Far away. Where no one talks about Dad's jeans."

But before she could escape, a familiar figure caught her eye at the booth's edge. Ruth Jenkins, wearing silver and beach glass earrings and a necklace that caught the afternoon light like trapped stars.

"Those are stunning," a woman was saying, reaching toward Ruth's ear. "Which booth did you get them from? I need a pair."

Ruth's hand flew to her earring, protective. "Oh, I —I made them."

The woman's eyes widened. "You made them? Do you have others? Are you selling?"

Carl Jenkins looked up from his phone—actually looked up—surprise flickering across his face.

"They're just a hobby," Ruth started, but something shifted in her expression. Maybe it was the festival air. Maybe it was the magic of the lynx. "But yes. I have others."

"Where's your booth?"

"I don't—" Ruth paused, straightened. "I'll be at the inn tomorrow morning. In the parlor. Someone else asked to see my collection earlier, so I'm doing a small showing. You could come by. Around ten?"

"Perfect!" The woman turned to her companion. "Did you hear that? Handmade jewelry at the inn!"

Carl stared at his wife like he'd never seen her before.

Ruth didn't notice. She was watching the woman walk away, her hand touching her earring with something that looked like pride.

Katie caught Ruth's eye and smiled. Ruth smiled back.

The afternoon whiled itself away in sensation. Sun hot on her shoulders. Kids' delighted gasps at the welding demonstration. The taste of Stan Murphy's inexplicably excellent barbecue. Music from the main stage, covers of songs everyone knew, everyone singing along off-key and perfect.

But under it all, awareness of Graham.

Graham helping Mrs. Frankl with her Historical Society display.

Graham lifting boxes like they weighed nothing.

Graham laughing—actually laughing—at something Captain Bernie said.

Graham's eyes finding hers across the crowd, again and again, like magnets discovering their match.

The sun was starting its slow descent when the music shifted. The band had rested up, but apparently not enough. Either that or they thought the Dune Festival needed a set of slow, sappy songs.

"Time to dance!" Ella appeared at Katie's elbow, flushed and happy from her own booth's success. "Come on!"

"I don't—"

"Everyone dances at the festival."

It was true. The street had been cleared in front of the stage, and couples were already swaying. The Kowalskis, married forty years, still looking at each other like newlyweds. Captain Bernie with Agnes, both pretending they weren't pleased about it. Even her parents, her father's hand gentle on her mother's back.

"I'll watch," Katie said.

"You'll dance."

Graham's voice, behind her. Close behind her.

She turned. He stood there in the golden light, those ridiculous jeans and that perfect shirt, hand extended.

"I don't really know how," she admitted.

"Neither do I." His smile was self-deprecating and sincere. "We'll figure it out."

His hand was warm. Callused from books, which shouldn't have been possible but was. He led her to the makeshift dance floor, found a spot where the evening sun hit just right, turning everything amber, royal purple, and possible.

"Hand here," he said, placing hers on his shoulder.

She could feel the heat of him through cotton. Feel the solid reality of him.

His hand found her waist, careful but certain.

"Now we just..." He moved, and she moved with him, and suddenly they were dancing.

Not well. Graham really didn't know how, kept

trying to lead with the wrong foot, overcorrecting into stumbles. But he laughed at himself, and she laughed with him, and then they found something that wasn't quite dancing but wasn't quite not.

"You came to my presentation," she said into his shoulder.

"Of course I did."

"You sat in the front row."

"Best view."

She pulled back to look at him. "Graham."

"Katie."

The way he said her name. Like it was the only word that mattered.

The song shifted, something even slower. Graham adjusted, pulled her closer. She could feel his heartbeat, faster than his calm expression suggested.

"I broke up with Finn," she said. "Not that we were together. But the idea of it. The possibility."

"I know."

"How?"

"I had to go up to the inn for Agnes. The sand globe. It's been golden all afternoon."

She laughed against his shirt. "The inn's gossip network."

"The best kind." His hand tightened slightly on her waist. "Are you okay?"

"More than okay."

They swayed, finding rhythm that had nothing to do with music. Around them, Green Arbor danced and laughed and celebrated being exactly what it was. But Katie's world had narrowed to this: Graham's hand in hers. Graham's breath against her hair. Graham's body, solid and real and here.

"Katie."

She looked up. His eyes behind his glasses were dark, intense in a way she'd never seen. Or never let herself see.

"I need to tell you something," he said.

Her heart hammered against her ribs.

"I—"

"Katie!"

They sprang apart like guilty teenagers. Finn stood at the edge of the dance floor, still perfect in his calculated casual wear, looking at them like they were a problem to solve.

"We need to discuss tomorrow," he said to Katie, ignoring Graham entirely. "The presentation. I've reconsidered our approach."

"There is no 'our,'" Katie said.

"Don't be childish." His patience was gone now, replaced by something harder. "The Pellingers are expecting—"

"The Pellingers can expect whatever they want." Graham's voice was still calm, but Katie felt the tension in his body. "Katie's made her decision."

Finn's gaze shifted to Graham, dismissive. "This doesn't concern you."

"Actually, it does." Graham stepped slightly forward. Not aggressive. Just... present. "Everything concerning Katie concerns me."

The words landed like stones in water, ripples spreading.

Katie stared at him. Finn stared at him. Half the festival stared at him.

Graham's ears went red, but he didn't back down.

"Katie," Finn said, trying to reclaim control. "Be realistic. What can this place offer you? What can he offer you?"

"Everything that matters," Katie said, surprised by her own certainty.

Finn's perfect face twisted into something less perfect. "You're making a mistake."

"Maybe." She reached for Graham's hand, found it already reaching for hers. "But it's mine to make."

Finn left. Just turned and walked away, out of the festival, out of Green Arbor's orbit, out of Katie's story.

"Did you mean it?" she asked Graham. "Everything concerning me concerns you?"

His ears were still red, but his eyes were steady. "I've meant it for five years."

Five years.

"Graham—"

"I know." His thumb traced circles on her palm. "Wrong timing. Always wrong timing. But Katie, I—"

"Everybody to the beach!" Liam's voice boomed across the festival. "Fireworks in ten minutes!"

The moment shattered. People moved toward the beach for better views. But Graham didn't let go of her hand.

"After?" he asked.

"After," she promised.

They walked to the beach together, fingers intertwined, Katie's entire body humming with possibility. The sand was cool under her feet—when had she taken off her shoes?—and the lake stretched endless and patient.

The first firework exploded overhead, gold and white and perfect.

Graham pulled her back against his chest, arms wrapping around her waist. She could feel him breathing. Feel his heartbeat. Feel the solid, steady truth of him.

"I see you," he whispered into her hair, words almost lost under the boom of fireworks. "I've always seen you."

Katie turned in his arms, looked up at his face painted in explosive light.

"I'm starting to see you too."

His eyes dropped to her mouth. Her breath caught.

The world narrowed to this moment, this possibility, this—

The grand finale erupted overhead, thirty seconds of pure light and sound, and everyone cheered.

Including Emma Hartwell, who appeared at their knees, sticky with cotton candy and vibrating with sugar rush.

"That was amazing! Katie, are you Graham's girlfriend now? Mom says you should be. She says it's about time. Are you going to get married? Can I be in the wedding?"

Graham's laugh rumbled through his chest. "Slow down, Emma."

"But are you?" She looked between them with six-year-old intensity.

Katie met Graham's eyes over Emma's head. Saw promise there. Patience there. Everything there.

"We're figuring it out," she said.

Emma considered this. "Okay. But figure it out fast. I start second grade in September."

She ran off, leaving them standing in the aftermath of fireworks and feelings.

"Walk you home?" Graham asked.

"Well, to my truck."

They left the festival still humming behind them. Walked the quiet streets, hands linked, everything different and everything exactly the same.

At her her truck, moths dancing in the hardware store's back light, Graham stopped.

"Tomorrow," he said. "The presentation. Whatever happens—"

"I know."

He cupped her face in his hands, thumbs tracing her cheekbones. For a moment, she thought he would kiss her. Wanted him to kiss her with an intensity that surprised her.

Instead, he pressed his lips to her forehead. Gentle. Reverent. Promise.

"Tomorrow," he said again.

"Tomorrow."

She watched him walk away, those impossible jeans and that perfect shirt disappearing into the dark.

At the cottage, her workshop waited. The lighthouse sculpture, complete now, honest and angry and true. Her presentation, ready. Her choice, made.

But tonight wasn't for metal and fire.

Tonight was for lying in the dark, replaying the weight of Graham's arms around her. The rumble of his laugh through his chest. The way he'd said I've meant it for five years like he was confessing to a crime and offering absolution at once.

She touched her forehead where he'd kissed her. The spot still burned, a brand that marked her as someone worth seeing. Someone worth waiting for.

Five years.

How had she not known? How had she not seen?

Maybe because she'd been too busy looking else-where—at galleries that didn't want her, at dreams that didn't fit, at men like Finn who saw her as raw material rather than finished art.

While Graham had been there all along. Seeing her. Steady as lighthouse beam, patient as lake waves, constant as the poetry section's rebellion.

Tomorrow would bring presentations and decisions and consequences.

But tonight, Katie Carter lay in the dark and let herself feel the truth of it: Graham Cheever wanted her. Had wanted her for years.

The poetry section was definitely plotting something.

And for the first time in her life, so was her heart.

Chapter Sixteen

The Inn's conference room smelled like judgment and lemon polish.

Katie stood to the side of the open door, her giant Rubbermaid tub clutched against her chest like armor that had already failed. Through the wood, she could hear murmured voices—the committee arranging themselves, papers shuffling, the particular quality of quiet that preceded verdicts.

Her good jeans felt too stiff. The white button-down she'd borrowed from her mother pulled across her shoulders. Even her hair, twisted into something resembling professional, threatened rebellion.

In her pocket, a folded piece of paper. Graham had left it on her truck windshield that morning, held down by a rock from the beach. Page 73 from the poetry book, carefully torn out:

"Truth is the only foundation
That holds when storms come.
Build there."

Build there.

Easy for dead poets to say.

Mrs. Frankl stepped out, in purple so deep it was almost black, her expression unreadable as lake ice.

"There you are," she said. "We're ready."

The conference room had been transformed. Gone was the warm chaos of wedding planning or casual meetings. The table gleamed like accusation. Five committee members arranged along one side like a tribunal. The projector screen pulled down, waiting for visions.

Graham sat at the far end, glasses catching window light so she couldn't see his eyes.

He didn't look at her.

Finn already occupied one of the two chairs set for presenters. Of course he'd arrived early, claimed territory. His laptop open, his smile ready, his clothes calculated to suggest artist-who-could-also-attend-galas.

"Katie." He nodded like they were colleagues.

Like he hadn't tried to colonize her vision.

Like she hadn't walked away from him yesterday.

She took the empty chair, its legs scraping against wood in a sound that made everyone wince.

"Mr. Davidson will present first," Mrs. Frankl announced. "Fifteen minutes, followed by questions. Then Ms. Carter."

Finn stood with water flowing downhill confidence. His presentation began exactly as Katie expected—sleek images flowing across the screen, his voice painting pictures of Green Arbor transformed into an arts destination.

Then her work appeared.

Not mentioned. Not referenced. Just there.

Her lighthouse sculpture filled the screen, photographed from her workshop—when had he taken this?—presented as part of "the collaborative vision for integrated arts programming."

Her metalworking techniques, described in language she recognized because she'd texted it to him, now emerging from his mouth as "our innovative approach to traditional crafts."

Our.

The committee leaned forward, interested. Captain Bernie took notes. Jim Hartwell nodded.

Graham's jaw had gone tight, but he stayed silent.

The conference room developed weather. Not dramatically—just a subtle drop in pressure that made everyone's ears pop, a rattle at the windows, a chill that raised goosebumps despite the June warmth outside.

Mrs. Frankl pulled her purple jacket closer. Jim Hartwell rubbed his arms.

The projector flickered. Once. Twice. Finn's stolen images of Katie's sketches stuttered on the screen like the building itself was trying to reject them.

"Technical difficulties?" Captain Bernie muttered.

More images. Her sketches for the interpretive displays, photographed over her shoulder at the town hall. Her workshop layout, which he'd somehow mapped. Her community program, repackaged with ceramic additions.

Her entire vision, swallowed into his.

"Questions?" Mrs. Frankl asked when he finished.

"Impressive integration of local elements," Jim said. "This metalwork especially. When did you develop these techniques?"

"The technique development has been a collaborative process," Finn said smoothly. "Green Arbor's artists have been incredibly generous with their knowledge."

Generous.

Like she'd offered it.

Like it had been hers to give and she'd chosen to.

Katie's hands clenched in her lap. Her mother's shirt pulled tighter.

"Ms. Carter," Mrs. Frankl said. "Your presentation."

Katie stood on legs that felt like water. Walked to the

front. Opened the lid of her giant rubber tub and pulled out her portfolio.

Her original sketches looked amateur after Finn's digital display. Her handwritten notes seemed childish. Her photographs—just printed at the drugstore—felt like elementary school show-and-tell.

She could give her prepared presentation. Talk about her vision that Finn had already stolen. Try to claim ownership of ideas he'd just presented better.

Or.

"He stole my work," she said.

The words dropped into the room like metal into still water. The windows that had been rattling stilled. Even the air seemed to hold its breath, waiting.

Silence.

Then chaos.

"That's a serious accusation," Jim Hartwell said.

"Those were my sketches," Katie continued, voice steadier than her hands. "My techniques. My programs. Photographed without permission and presented as collaboration that never existed."

Finn's face rearranged itself into wounded surprise. "Katie, we discussed these ideas over dinner. Naturally, there would be overlap—"

"You took photos of my work without asking. Or crediting."

"Documentation of the evaluation process—"

"You quoted my texts word for word."

Now she wondered if he even did his own ceramics. He hadn't brought any, only those professional-grade photos.

The committee shifted, uncomfortable. Mrs. Frankl's mouth had become a thin line.

"This is highly irregular," she said.

"What's irregular," Katie said, heat rising in her chest, "is someone with no connection to this place taking ownership of work that grew from it."

"Ms. Carter," Mayor Thompson warned.

But Katie was done being warned.

"Look at his presentation again. Every local element—whose work is it? Every community connection—who made it? He's not bringing art to Green Arbor. He's taking it from us."

"These are serious allegations," Jim said. "Do you have proof?"

Proof.

Her word against his polish.

"The timestamps on my sketches—"

"Which could have been added later," Finn interjected smoothly. "Katie, I understand you're upset about yesterday, but turning this into a personal attack—"

"Personal?"

"Perhaps," Finn said, voice dripping reason, "Ms.

Carter's judgment has been compromised. After all, she does have a certain... advantage in this competition."

The room temperature dropped ten degrees.

"Advantage?" Mrs. Frankl's voice could have frozen flame.

"Graham Cheever is on this committee." Finn's eyes found Graham, dismissive and accusatory at once. "And as everyone at the festival witnessed, he and Ms. Carter are... involved."

Involved.

Katie looked at Graham. He'd gone completely still, face carved from stone.

"Ridiculous," she started.

"Is it?" Finn pulled out his phone, swiped to a photo. Katie and Graham dancing, her head on his shoulder. Another swipe. Graham's arms around her during fireworks. Another. The forehead kiss. "The festival was quite... illuminating."

"Mr. Cheever," Mrs. Frankl said, each word precise as a blade. "Is there a personal relationship that would compromise your objectivity?"

Graham stood slowly. Removed his glasses. Cleaned them with mechanical precision.

"I recuse myself."

Three words. Quiet. Final.

"Graham—" Katie started.

"It's appropriate." He didn't look at her. Wouldn't look at her. "My objectivity could be questioned."

Could be.

Not was.

Could be.

Like he was stepping back from possibility itself.

"I'll wait outside," he said to Mrs. Frankl. Then, finally, to Katie: "The beach stairs. Behind the inn."

He left, the door closing with a soft click that sounded like a goodbye.

Katie stood alone at the front of the room, portfolio useless in her hands, committee staring at her like she'd broken something irreparable.

"Well," Finn said, satisfaction poorly disguised as concern. "Perhaps we should continue?"

"Ms. Carter," Mrs. Frankl said. "Do you wish to proceed with your presentation?"

Did she?

Graham had left. Recused himself. Stepped back like he always did, careful distance restored.

But he'd told her where.

The beach stairs.

Build there, the poem had said.

Truth as foundation.

Katie straightened her mother's shirt. Set down her portfolio. Bent over and pulled out not her prepared presentation but the angry lighthouse sculpture, wrapped in cloth.

"This is my work."

She unwrapped it slowly, metal catching the afternoon light. It was ugly and honest and absolutely itself.

"I made this while trying to be something else. Someone else. It insisted on being true instead."

She looked at each committee member except the empty space where Graham should have been.

"Finn Davidson is talented. Connected. Sophisticated. He could make Green Arbor famous. Or he could leave tomorrow for greener pastures."

Deep breath.

"He doesn't see us. He sees opportunity. He doesn't hear our stories. He hears content. He doesn't understand that the lighthouse isn't just a building. It's a promise. And promises should be kept by people who understand their weight."

She set the sculpture on the table. It scraped against wood, harsh and real.

"I don't have a laptop presentation. I don't have gallery connections. I don't have sophisticated vocabulary for what I do. I have fire and metal and thirty years of loving that lighthouse. That's all."

She gathered her portfolio, leaving the sculpture on the table like evidence.

"Thank you for your consideration."

She walked to the door, hand on the handle when Mrs. Frankl spoke.

"Ms. Carter. The committee will need time to deliberate."

Katie nodded without turning.

Outside, the inn's hallway stretched toward the back door, toward the beach stairs, toward Graham.

Toward another conversation she wasn't ready for.

Behind her, she heard Finn's voice, smooth and confident, already reshaping the narrative.

Ahead, June sunshine and Graham's careful distance and the possibility that she'd just lost everything.

Katie walked toward it anyway.

Truth as foundation.

Even when it meant standing alone.

Chapter Seventeen

Graham Cheever sat on the third step from the bottom of the beach stairs, where five years of foot traffic had worn the wood smooth as lies.

Lake Michigan stretched before him, that particular shade of blue-green that had no name in his mental filing system. Somewhere between Turquoise (subcategory: Unattainable) and Cobalt (subcategory: Katie's Eyes When Angry). The waves breathed against the shore, patient and eternal and completely unconcerned with the fact that his entire organizational structure was collapsing.

Sand had infiltrated his dress shoes. The expensive ones he'd worn to seem professional, objective, worthy of making decisions about other people's futures. Now the fine grains worked between his toes like tiny accusations. His jacket lay abandoned on the top crossbeam of the wooden railing. His tie, yanked off the moment he'd cleared the inn's back door, was wadded in its pocket like a resignation letter.

The sun pressed hot against his back through the white dress shirt that had seemed so appropriate this morning. Appropriate. Katie was right. His favorite word. His favorite armor.

Filed under: Cowardice (subcategory: Disguised As Wisdom).

Except the filing system wasn't working anymore. Everything scattered, mixed, bled together. Five years of careful categorization dissolving like sugar in rain.

His hands shook.

Graham Cheever's hands never shook. He catalogued, analyzed, shelved emotions like books. He maintained professional distance. He recused himself.

He recused himself.

"I recuse myself."

His own voice, steady and dead as winter lake.

Katie's face.

Filed under: Mistakes (subcategory: Irrevocable).

No. Filed under: Patterns (subcategory: Hereditary).

No. Filed under—

Nothing. There was no file for this. No category for

walking away from the one person who made his careful world worth maintaining.

The lake breeze swept up the bluff, carrying the scent of water and the illusion of speed. It rattled the dune grass—marram grass, his mind supplied automatically, *Ammophila breviligulata*, because even in crisis he couldn't stop cataloging. The grass whispered secrets in a language he'd never learned, probably about men who chose truth over safety.

Below, the beach stretched a couple of miles, dotted with families. Grownups on beach towels and under umbrellas, kids in and out of the surf. Normal people doing normal things, not sitting on stairs reconsidering every choice they'd made since they were twenty-seven.

Five years.

He could pinpoint the exact moment: December 23rd, Katie home from Chicago for Christmas. She'd entered the bookstore covered in metal shavings that caught the light like fallen stars. Looking for books on patina techniques, she'd said, her voice rough like she'd been crying or breathing fire.

He'd had seven different options for her.

"You're like a book GPS, Graham Cheever," she'd laughed, the sound warming his sleepy store. His careful life. His creative soul.

He should have said something then. When her defenses were down, when she needed an anchor.

Instead, he'd ordered eight more books on metalworking and filed his feelings under: Inappropriate (subcategory: Timing).

Then she'd stayed. One month became two became five years of watching her date men who arrived in June and left by September. Men who saw her as a summer adventure, a small-town story to tell at dinner parties. While Graham ordered books she didn't know she needed and made coffee exactly how she liked it and tried not to memorize the way afternoon light caught in her hair.

Filed under: Pathetic (subcategory: Increasingly So).

The wooden decking creaked above him. Not the settling of sun-warmed wood, but footsteps. Hesitant. Stop. Continue. Stop again.

His body responded without permission. Every muscle tightening, heart attempting escape through his ribs, breathing suddenly manual and failing.

She appeared at the top of the stairs, backlit by afternoon sun that turned her into something mythical. Hair escaping its attempted professionalism in wisps that caught the light. Her mother's shirt pulled wrong across her shoulders.

Nothing in her hands. What had happened to her portfolio?

Katie descended slowly, each step deliberate on the sun-bleached wood. The stairs complained under her weight—not much, she was small, but they'd been here since the seventies and had opinions about everything. She sat exactly one step above him. Not beside. The space between them measurable in inches, infinite in meaning.

She smelled like metal and inn furniture polish and underneath, the particular scent that was just Katie—something warm and dangerous, like a forge before it fired.

"You left."

Not a question. An accusation that landed between his shoulder blades.

"It was appropriate."

"Appropriate." She laughed, but it had edges. "Your favorite word."

Something in Graham's chest cracked. Not gently, like ice in spring, but sharp, sudden, structural. He turned to look at her straight.

"What was I supposed to do? Sit there while he made it sound cheap?"

The words surprised them both. No filing system, no careful consideration, just raw truth spilling like blood from a fresh cut.

"Five years, Katie." His hands clenched on his knees, knuckles white as exposed bone. "Five years of watching you date summer people who didn't know you hate pistachio ice cream but eat it anyway to be polite. Five years of hearing how dull everything in this town was. And everyone."

He stood abruptly, couldn't sit still, couldn't contain this in the narrow space of wooden steps. He took the final steps to the small pine and cord landing. Sand ground under his dress shoes as he paced the tiny landing. The lake spread endless before him, but his world had shrunk to this: Katie on the stairs, watching him unravel.

"Five years of cataloging every smile, every time you touched my hand reaching for change, every time you said my name like it meant something more than just the guy who sells books." He laughed, bitter as February wind. "Filed under: Pathetic. Subcategory: Increasingly So."

"You never said anything." Her voice was small, confused. "How was I supposed to know?"

"Because I'm careful. Controlled. Appropriate." He spat his favorite word like spoiled milk. "I don't say things. I maintain distance. I recuse myself. Apparently, from my own life."

The wind picked up, sending sand swirling around them. It stuck to his skin, gathered in the corners of his eyes, filled his mouth with the taste of earth and patience worn thin. Behind him, the waves crashed harder against the shore, foam white as the lies he'd told himself about noble self-sacrifice.

"I've been writing a book," he said, the confession ripping from somewhere deep. "A thriller. The protagonist, Jake Morrison, he's brave. He takes chances. He doesn't recuse himself when things get complicated."

Graham's glasses were filthy with sand and fingerprints. He cleaned them with mechanical precision, needing the familiar action while his world reorganized itself.

"I've been writing the man I want to be while being the coward I am."

"You're not a coward." Katie stood too, invaded his space, got close enough that he could see the gold flecks in her eyes that appeared only in direct sunlight. "A coward wouldn't have stayed. Wouldn't have been there every time I needed something."

"A coward is exactly what I am." The words tasted true, bitter and necessary. "My father was an alcoholic. Charming, brilliant, completely unreliable. He wanted things so badly he destroyed them. My mother, our family, himself eventually."

The admission hung between them while the lake continued its eternal conversation with the shore. A gull cried overhead, probably mocking his emotional spillage.

"I catalog and file and maintain distance because I'm terrified of being him. Of wanting something so much I ruin it."

Katie stepped closer. Close enough that he could feel the heat radiating from her skin, sun-warmed and alive.

"You're not your father."

"How do you know?"

"Because you've had five years to destroy us and instead you protected it. Protected something that didn't even exist yet."

The space between them vibrated with possibility. Graham's hand rose without permission, almost touched her face, stopped an inch from her cheek. The distance felt like miles, like years, like every careful choice he'd ever made.

"Katie, if we start this, I won't be appropriate. I won't be careful."

"Good."

One word. Simple. Devastating.

They were breathing the same air now, existing in the same space they'd been dancing around for years. The sun tucked itself behind a cumulus cloud, streaking everything gold. Graham could kiss her. Right now. Could close that last inch and—

"Katie?"

Ella's voice from above, urgent.

"The committee's made a decision."

Already?

The moment shattered like safety glass, small pieces

that couldn't cut but left you knowing something whole had broken.

Katie pulled back, reality flooding her face. She had to go. Had to hear whether she'd won or lost. Whether her truth had been enough.

"Whatever happens," Graham said, his voice rough as sand-scraped wood, "I'll be here."

"Still recused?"

"Not from us." The words came from that new, raw place where his filing system used to live. "Never from us."

She ran up the stairs, taking them two at a time, boots thundering on wood. At the top, she paused, turned back. Silhouetted against the afternoon sky, hair wild with wind and escape, she looked like something from mythology. A goddess of fire and metal and second chances.

"Graham?"

"Yeah?"

"You're as brave as Jake."

She disappeared, leaving only the echo of her footsteps and the lingering scent of possibility.

Graham sat back down on the third step, harder than intended. His legs had gone liquid, bones optional. Everything he'd carefully organized for thirty-two years lay in ruins around him. No files. No categories. No professional distance.

Just truth, raw and terrifying and absolutely necessary.

He pulled out his phone, opened the manuscript he'd been hiding for three years. His fingers moved without thought, without plan, without careful consideration.

Chapter Nineteen

Jake Morrison was done being careful.

He stood up, straightened his tie, and walked back into the room where everything that mattered waited.

"I don't recuse myself," he said. "Not from this. Not from her. Not anymore."

Because some things were worth the risk of wanting too much.

Some things were worth destroying yourself to build.

Some things were worth filing under Now instead of Later.

Graham stood, sand cascading from his slacks. His glasses were filthy again. His shirt was untucked. His carefully controlled world had completely collapsed.

He'd never felt more certain of anything in his life.

Whatever the committee had decided, his decision was made.

No more filing under Later (subcategory: When It's Safe).

Everything filed under Now (subcategory: Finally).

He climbed the stairs toward the inn, toward Katie, toward whatever came next.

The lake breathed its approval behind him, waves applauding against the shore. Even the dune grass seemed to whisper encouragement, or maybe that was just the blood rushing in his ears, the sound of a careful man finally, finally choosing to be brave.

Chapter Eighteen

The inn's conference room door weighed a thousand pounds.

Katie stood outside it, hand on the brass knob worn smooth by decades of verdicts. Through the wood came murmuring—committee voices low and serious, papers shuffling like leaves, someone's throat clearing in that way that preceded life-changing announcements.

Graham wasn't in there.

Recused. Maintaining his careful distance when it mattered most.

No. Not when it mattered most.

He'd grabbed her heart with both hands.

She turned the knob.

Four faces turned toward her. Mrs. Frankl in that so-deep purple. Jim Hartwell's pen poised over his notepad like a sword waiting to fall. Captain Bernie, his tie nearly fully undone. Dottie Kowalski with her teacher's concerned face —the one that could mean pride or disappointment.

The empty chair at the table's end, screaming Graham's absence.

"Ms. Carter." Mrs. Frankl's voice carried the formal weight of ceremony. "Please sit."

The chair scraped against wood—fingernails on a chalkboard, a sound like resistance.

"The committee has reached a decision."

Katie's hands found each other in her lap, fingers weaving complicated knots. Her mother's shirt, soaked with sweat, stuck to her spine. The air in the room felt thick, hard to pull into lungs that had forgotten their purpose.

"After careful consideration of both presentations, the demonstrated skills, and the vision for Green Arbor's lighthouse..."

The pause stretched. Taffy-pulled. Torture.

"We've selected you for the position."

The words hit her like a wave—first knocking her breathless, then lifting her, carrying her somewhere she'd never dared believe she could reach. Her vision blurred. Not tears. Not yet. Just the world reorganizing itself around this impossible truth: they'd chosen her. Her messy, angry, honest self.

Katie blinked hard. The committee watched her with expressions ranging from satisfaction (Captain Bernie) to careful pleasure (Mrs. Frankl).

"I—what?"

"Your passion is undeniable," Mrs. Frankl continued, the faintest smile warming her formal facade. "Your connection to this community, your practical skills, and yes, your artistic vision make you the right choice for Green Arbor's lighthouse."

Katie's chest cracked open, flooding with something that felt like sunrise. "But Finn—his presentation—"

"Was polished," Jim Hartwell said. "Professional. Impressive, even. But the lighthouse doesn't need impressive. It needs someone who understands what it means to us."

The door burst open.

Finn stood there, phone clutched like a trophy, face alight.

"Apologies for the interruption," he said, not sounding sorry at all. His expensive cologne preceded him into the room, too strong, like confidence worn as armor. "But I've just received extraordinary news."

He moved into the room with his usual flowing grace, but Katie caught something different in his posture. Lighter. Like a weight had lifted.

"Mr. Davidson," Mrs. Frankl said, voice cooling several degrees. "We've just informed Ms. Carter of our decision."

"Ah." Finn's smile was brilliant, practiced, and somehow genuinely pleased. "Congratulations, Katie. Truly."

Katie stared at him. This wasn't the reaction of someone who'd lost.

"The timing is actually perfect," Finn continued, holding up his phone. "I've just been awarded the Krasnoff Prize. Rather prestigious. Comes with a teaching position at NYU starting next fall semester."

Understanding dawned like cold water.

He was relieved.

"You knew," Katie said, the words coming without thought. "You knew about the prize during presentations."

Finn's smile flickered. Just for a second. But she saw it.

"The committee made the right choice," he said smoothly. "Your connection to this place is... authentic. And now I'm free to pursue opportunities more suited to my trajectory."

More suited.

Like the lighthouse had been beneath him all along.

"The position was a two-year commitment," Captain Bernie rumbled, eyes narrowing.

"Which I would have honored, of course." Finn's lie was beautiful, polished as his shoes. "But perhaps the universe knew better. Katie gets her lighthouse, I get New York. Everyone wins."

Katie stood, legs steady as iron. "You would have taken both if you could."

Finn's mask slipped, just slightly. "The art world requires flexibility."

"The art world," Katie said, tasting the words like copper. "The real world requires truth. And the truth is you were never going to stay. This was only ever a consolation prize for you. A backup plan."

Finn straightened his already-straight collar. "I wish you the best with your... lighthouse. I'm sure the tourists will love your little metalwork demonstrations."

Little.

The word hung in the air like a slur.

"Get out." Mrs. Frankl's voice could have frozen July. "Now."

Finn left with the same flowing grace he'd entered with, but Katie caught the truth in his hurried steps. He'd wanted both—the prestige of the prize and the resume line of the lighthouse. Losing the lighthouse meant he couldn't have everything.

For someone like Finn, that was its own kind of failure.

"Well," Dottie said into the silence, "that was illuminating."

Captain Bernie snorted. "Boy would've turned our lighthouse into his personal stepping stone."

"Committee made the right choice," Jim said, closing his notepad with finality. "Ms. Carter, Katie, the lighthouse keeper position is yours. Two-year minimum commitment, with the possibility of extension. The cottage and studio are included. You can move in next month."

Next month.

A home. A studio. A purpose.

Everything.

"Thank you," Katie managed through a throat gone tight with emotion.

They filed out, each offering congratulations. Captain Bernie actually hugged her, an embrace colored with pipe tobacco and, maybe, rum. Dottie squeezed her hands. Even Jim Hartwell smiled.

Finally, alone in the conference room, Katie let herself breathe. Let herself feel it.

She'd won.

Not because Graham had fought for her—he'd stayed recused.

Not because Finn had withdrawn—he'd already lost.

Because she'd stood there with her angry sculpture and her truth and been enough.

"Katie?"

Mrs. Frankl stood in the doorway.

"Your young man is probably still on the beach stairs. Might want to share the good news."

Your young man.

Heat flooded Katie's face, but she nodded.

The inn's hallway stretched toward escape. The sand globe swirled gold, celebrating. Through the parlor, where Mrs. Jenkins was showing a gorgeous necklace to a very interested trio of women. Through the back door, where the clouds had parted, and the sunshine fell like benediction.

Graham sat exactly where she'd left him. Third step from the bottom. Head in his hands. Dress shoes full of sand. Looking like a man awaiting execution.

He heard her coming.

Stood.

Turned.

His face—hope and fear and everything between.

"I got it," she said.

Two words that changed his entire geography. Joy remade him, transformed careful Graham into something incandescent.

"Katie."

Just her name.

Everything.

She flew down the stairs. He climbed up. Time stretched like heated metal. Each step felt eternal and too fast. She could see everything—the way sand had dried in his hair, making it stick up at impossible angles. The wrinkles in his shirt where he'd been hunched forward. The way his hands shook as he reached for her.

This was Graham. Her Graham. Who'd waited five years and was still shaking as he touched her.

They met in the middle, and finally—finally—neither stepped back.

His hands came up to frame her face, thumbs tracing her cheekbones with reverence that made her chest ache.

"I'm sorry I wasn't there," he said. "I should have—"

"You stayed recused," Katie said, understanding flooding through her. "You let me win it myself."

"You didn't need me to."

"No," she agreed. "But I wanted you there anyway."

Something shifted in his eyes. Heat replacing careful distance.

"Katie."

"Graham."

They were sharing the same air, existing in the same moment, no more filing systems or careful categories between them.

"If I kiss you now," he said, voice thick, "I won't be appropriate about it."

"Good," she said, and pulled him down to her.

His mouth on hers was revelation. All that careful control shattered into something desperate and tender and absolutely perfect. He kissed like he'd been waiting years—because he had. She kissed him back like she'd finally come home—because she had.

He tasted like coffee and possibility. Like every book he'd ever ordered for her, every smile he'd tried to hide, every moment he'd stepped back when he wanted to step forward. His hands shook against her face—Graham's steady hands, finally unsteady.

She made a sound—sob or laugh, she couldn't tell—and he swallowed it, pulled her closer, kissed her like he was memorizing her, cataloging her, filing her under "Forever."

Around them, the world noticed. A window creaked open above—Ella probably, or Agnes, or the inn itself wanting a better view. Someone cheered from the beach.

But Katie noticed none of it. Her world had narrowed to this: Graham's mouth on hers, Graham's heart hammering against her chest, Graham finally—finally—not being careful. His hands tangled in her hair. Hers fisted in his sand-covered shirt. The sun painted them gold. The lake sang approval.

They broke apart only when oxygen became necessary, foreheads pressed together, breathing hard.

"Five years," he said against her mouth.

"Five years," she agreed, then kissed him again.

Because they had time now.

All the time in the world.

"About damn time!"

Captain Bernie's voice boomed from the inn's porch above.

Katie pulled back just enough to laugh against her mouth. "We have an audience."

"Let them watch," Graham said, and kissed her again.

Because Green Arbor had been waiting for this as long as they had.

Chapter Nineteen

The lighthouse cottage workshop smelled like pumpkins and acetylene. Halloween week, that last odd warm week before the winter winds really stepped in.

Katie stood back from her latest piece—not a lighthouse this time, but a wave caught mid-break, copper and steel twisted into something that looked like it might crash any second. Commissioned by the maritime museum downstate. Her third commission this month.

Amazing what happened when you stopped apologizing for your work.

Late afternoon light slanted through the windows, that particular October gold that turned everything it touched into treasure. Lake Michigan visible through every window, moody today, grey-green and white-capped. The foghorn would sound tonight. She could feel it in the air pressure, the way the wind kept shifting.

Footsteps on the cottage path. Not tourists—the lighthouse closed at four outside of the summer season. Not the careful tread of visitors anyway, but the confident stride of someone who belonged.

Graham.

Her body recognized him before her brain caught up, that pleasant flutter in her stomach that hadn't faded in four months. Four months of Graham not being careful. Four months of discovering what that meant.

He shouldered through the workshop door, arms full of boxes that should have looked heavy but somehow didn't. He'd started running with her in the mornings, along the beach, up the brutal dune climb. Katie had never been so in shape.

"Book delivery," he announced, setting the boxes in the only clear corner. "Also, Mrs. Patterson wants to know if you're taking winter workshop students."

"Already?" Katie pulled off her welding gloves, ran fingers through her hair. Probably had metal shavings in it. Graham didn't seem to mind anymore. "It's not even November."

"Winter comes fast." He moved into her space, natural as breathing now, hand finding her waist. "Speaking of which, the poetry section has opinions about your window display."

"The poetry section can—"

He kissed her. Middle of the afternoon, work hours, anyone could walk by and see. Graham Cheever kissing Katie Carter in the lighthouse workshop like it was normal. Like it was everyday.

It was.

"The books," she said against his mouth, "are not going to catalog themselves."

"Mmm." His thumb traced circles on her hip, right where her shirt had ridden up. "They're already organized. Maritime history, local authors, children's books about lighthouses. Twenty percent commission, as discussed."

"Twenty-five."

"Twenty-five." He smiled, that new smile he'd developed, the one without any careful in it. "Highway robbery."

"Girlfriend privileges."

The word still felt new. Girlfriend. Like they were teenagers instead of thirty-somethings who'd wasted five years being idiots.

Not wasted. Graham insisted on that. Prepared. They'd been preparing.

"Actually," he said, pulling back slightly, "I have news."

Something in his tone made Katie's chest tighten. Good or bad?

"Agent news."

Definitely good.

"Graham!"

"She wants the full manuscript. Said the sample chapters were—" He paused, ears going red. "Compelling and unique."

Katie grabbed his face, kissed him hard. "I told you! Didn't I tell you? Jake Morrison is going to—"

"Katie."

Captain Bernie's voice from the doorway, amused and apologetic. They sprang apart like they hadn't been together for months, like the whole town hadn't been taking bets on when they'd set the big date.

"Sailing group from Detroit just called in," Bernie said, pretending he hadn't seen anything. "Storm tomorrow, so they're in port up at Leelanau. Want to know if you can do a private showing tomorrow. Twenty people."

"Sure." Katie grabbed her calendar, the one Graham had bought her, color-coded and everything. She was becoming him. Or he was becoming her. They were becoming something new. "Eleven?"

"I'll tell them." Bernie turned to go, paused. "Oh, and Graham? Message from the Mayor. You're officially commanded to attend Carter Thanksgiving. No exceptions, no excuses, and—his words—'no trying to spend it alone with a book like last year.'"

Graham's ears went red. "I wasn't—"

"Son, we all saw you in the bookstore window last Thanksgiving, eating Chinese takeout and reading." Bernie's weathered face crinkled with amusement. "Margaret Carter nearly broke down the door to drag you to their table."

"She did break down the door," Graham muttered. "Metaphorically."

Katie turned to stare at him. "You spent last Thanksgiving alone?"

"I had a book."

"Graham."

"A really good book."

"Graham!"

Bernie chuckled. "Well, not this year. Katie's dad was very specific. Said to tell you resistance is futile, and if you don't show up, he's sending Katie's mother after you." He winked. "I'll see you both there. I never miss Margaret's stuffing."

Bernie left, whistling something that sounded suspiciously like a wedding march.

Katie turned into Graham's arms, hands flat against his chest. "You've been spending Thanksgivings alone?"

"Not alone. With books."

"Graham."

"And sometimes Chinese food."

She kissed him, soft and fierce at once. "Never again."

"Never again," he agreed against her mouth. His family might be gone, but hers had claimed him. The way Green Arbor claimed everyone who belonged.

His arms tightened around her. Outside, the lake breathed against the shore.

"I love you," Graham said into her hair. Simple. Certain. Categorically.

"I love you too."

They stood there in the workshop, surrounded by half-finished metal, boxes of books, the light dying into purple dusk. The cottage that was home now. The lighthouse that was hers to tend. The man who'd waited five years and would probably wait fifty more if needed.

But he didn't need to wait anymore.

Neither of them did.

"Help me with the display?" Katie asked, pulling back. "If we're selling books, they should at least look good."

"The poetry section is going to have opinions."

"The poetry section always has opinions."

They unpacked books together as the sun dropped to sleep, as Green Arbor settled into autumn evening. Graham explaining his organization system, Katie immediately ignoring it in favor of what looked good. Him rolling his eyes but smiling. Her kissing the annoyance away.

Down the shore, lights began appearing in town. The hardware store's security light. The Roastery's warm windows. Above them, the inn glowing on its bluff.

Home.

All of it.

"Oh," Graham said, pulling out one last volume. "This one's not for sale."

Katie took it. *Women Who Work with Fire: Poems.* The same copy he'd given her months ago. But now there was an inscription on the title page, in Graham's careful writing:

For Katie, Who built herself from flame and iron, And taught me to stop being careful with my heart. All my love, Graham

Katie's vision blurred.

"Hey," Graham said, alarmed. "Are you—"

She kissed him quiet. Then kissed him loud. Then kissed him until the poetry section probably reorganized itself in scandal.

"Walk with me?" Katie asked, trying to catch her breath. "I need to check the lighthouse before dark."

They left the workshop, hands linked, walking the limestone pier that stretched into Lake Michigan like a promise kept in stone. The autumn wind whipped around them, carrying the scent of coming winter, of leaves turning, of the lake preparing for its chilliest moods.

A shadow moved through the dune grass—too large for a cat, too graceful for a dog.

Katie grabbed Graham's hand. "Did you see—?"

But the lynx, if it had been there at all, had already vanished into the growing dusk.

In front of them, Big Red—the Glen Arbor Light, technically—rose from its base with the solid certainty of first editions and promises kept. Forty feet of vermillion statement, that rusty color that photographers claimed was impossible to capture but which looked to him like October maples, like Katie's cheeks after working the forge, like urgency made visible.

Katie saw it differently. Those industrial bones—all that steel and iron, rivets like jewelry, the gallery railing wrought by hands that understood metal's moods.

"The light still works," she said, hand on the door. "Not officially, but the mechanism's intact."

Inside, their footsteps rang on metal stairs, echoing up the tower. Graham counted each step—habit—while Katie ran her hand along the wall, feeling the building's pulse through her palm.

At the top, the lamp room held the fading light like amber in glass. The lake spread in every direction, showing whitecaps like teeth.

"I'm adding sculptures to the gallery," Katie said, gesturing to the railing that circled the light. "Small ones that will cast shadows when the light sweeps through."

"I've been researching the original keeper's logs," Graham said. "Nicholas Harmon, 1889 to 1917. The flowering vine guy? He said they created a welcoming path for visitors and the souls of lost sailors."

Katie turned to him, the shadows making her eyes that shade of green that had no name in any filing system.

"We're really doing this," she said. "Keeping the lighthouse. Together."

"Together," he agreed, pulling her close.

Below them, Green Arbor spread like a map Graham could read, like a pattern Katie could forge. Their town. Their lighthouse.

"Home," Katie said.

"Home," Graham agreed.

And it was.

Also by Annika Stone

Green Arbor Stories

Room for Magic

Room for Light

Room for Dreams

The Room for Magic Trilogy

Sweet Romance

The Author Next Door

A Taste of Tradition

Lilac Hearts

A Melody for Sunshine

Level Up to Love

Cosmic Hearts

Wild Hearts of Yellowstone

The Christmas Cookie Trap

Winter's Gift

The Valentine's Ruse

About the Author

Annika Stone writes sweet contemporary romance where love shows up in unexpected places—small towns, big cities, magical inns, or ordinary Tuesdays. Her characters are everyday people with interesting lives, real problems, and hearts that recognize home when they find it. She's eternally hopeful, perpetually daydreaming, and absolutely certain everyone deserves their happy ending.

www.ingramcontent.com/pod-product-compliance
Lightning Source LLC
Chambersburg PA
CBHW060538190726
48283CB00003B/777